THE INCREDIBLE DIARY OF...

Fiction From The UK

Edited By Debbie Killingworth

First published in Great Britain in 2023 by:

Young Writers
Remus House
Coltsfoot Drive
Peterborough
PE2 9BF
Telephone: 01733 890066
Website: www.youngwriters.co.uk

All Rights Reserved
Book Design by Ashley Janson
© Copyright Contributors 2023
Softback ISBN 978-1-80459-956-3

Printed and bound in the UK by BookPrintingUK
Website: www.bookprintinguk.com
YB0565Z

Foreword

Dear Diary,

You will never guess what I did today! Shall I tell you? Some primary school pupils wrote some diary entries and I got to read them, and they were EXCELLENT!

Here at Young Writers we created some bright and funky worksheets along with fun and fabulous (and free) resources to help spark ideas and get inspiration flowing. And it clearly worked because WOW!! I can't believe the adventures I've been reading about. Real people, make-believe people, dogs and unicorns, even objects like pencils all feature and these diaries all have one thing in common – they are JAM-PACKED with imagination!

Here at Young Writers we want to pass our love of the written word onto the next generation and what better way to do that than to celebrate their writing by publishing it in a book! It sets their work free from homework books and notepads and puts it where it deserves to be – OUT IN THE WORLD!

Each awesome author in this book should be SUPER PROUD of themselves, and now they've got proof of their imagination, their ideas and their creativity in black and white, to look back on in years to come!

Contents

Akeley Wood Junior School, Wicken

Tommy Brook-Johnson (10)	1

Capenhurst CE Primary School, Capenhurst

Sophia Knowles (9)	3
Abigail Culbert (9)	4
E N (9)	6
Sophie Osborne (9)	8
Heidi-Rose Warmer (9)	10
Bella Ward (8)	11
Charlotte Rowson (8)	12
Riley Fisher (9)	13
Melia Burkey (8)	14
April Wells (8)	15
Emily Fereday (8)	16
Mia Rose (8)	17
William Riley (8)	18
Fletcher Swift (9)	19
Ruemu Edewor (8)	20
Orla Baxter (7)	21
Flynn Phillips (8)	22
Sophia Morris (9)	23
Verity Cottrell	24
Euan Metcalfe (9)	25
Mitchell Brown (9)	26
Nora Connor (8)	27
Finley Franks (8)	28
Penelope Smith Lum Wai (8)	29
Seb Dunbar (8)	30

Cotgrave Candleby Lane School, Cotgrave

Tilly Hird (9)	31
Freya Shread (8)	32
Grace Nickerson (9)	33
Eva Nembhard-Perry (8)	34
Josephine Grant (9)	35
Lily Skipp (8)	36

Deptford Park Primary School, Deptford

Amy Hoang (7)	37
Samuel Faux (7)	38
Aniyah D'Aguiar (7)	39
Kiro Osei-Poku Boakye (7)	40
Mahsheed Hurmat (8)	41
Nour Guendeba (7)	42
Anaiah Kasangu (7)	43
Jashaun Taylor (6)	44
Alexis Afrane-Ankama (7)	45
Skylar White (6)	46
Isaac Fernandes (6)	47
Israel-L Sarpong (7)	48
Eason Chen (7)	49
Maria Benzadi (7)	50
Emily Huang (6)	51
Jenny Tran (6)	52
Nelvin Afriyie (6)	53

Hadley Learning Community - Primary Phase, Hadley

Freddie Sheridon (8)   54
Isla Pollard (8)   56
Lamar Hammami (8)   57

Heathlands Primary School, Mansfield

Alesha Inskip (9)   58
Betty Allen (9)   60
Skye McCormack (9)   61
Freya Foster-Evans (9)   62
Corey Mitchell (9)   63
Odrija Baltina (8)   64
Layla Inskip (9)   65
Thomas Moss-Burton (9)   66
Aidan Brasil Ibhanesebhor (8)   67
Viktoria Lukasz (9)   68

Highwoods Academy, Mexborough

Henley Smith (9)   69
Kendall Goodyer (9)   70
Fareedah Hassan (9)   72
Lilly Hackford (9)   74
Vytis Karinauskas (9)   75
Lindsey-Rose (9)   76
Jacob Rix (8)   77
Mia Diggles (9)   78
Shillana Hibbins (9)   79
Ryan Fisher (9)   80

Seaton School, Aberdeen

Leah-Rose Wisniewska (9)   81
Piotr Bilinski (9)   82
Daniella Osakue (9)   83
Nadia Mikulska (8)   84
Nathan Bogdevic (8)   85
Zofia Uzar (8)   86
Orson Phillips (9)   87
Ambyr Brown (8)   88

Boti Bokor (9)   89
Lily Allen (9)   90
Jack Adams (9)   91

St Bede's RC Primary School, Denton Burn

Mylie Storey (11)   92
Amelia Wansell (11)   94
Amelia-Lily Mott (11)   96
Hannah Watson (11)   98
Lewis Allen (11)   99
Finley Wharton (11)   100
Libby Holden (11)   101
Olly Wright (10)   102
Katie Howard (11)   103
Atefa Aymon Zamil (11)   104
Michael Tait (11)   105
Paul Carling (11)   106
Jessica Nesbitt (11)   107

St John The Baptist CE Primary School, Worthing

Ryan Smart (10)   108
Noah Cane (10)   110
Benjamin Hoadley (10)   112
Joshua Gordon (9)   114
Delilah Gordon (9)   115
Delilah Fitt (9)   116
Mia Leaney (10)   117
Scarlett Ko (9)   118
Mia Franks (9)   119
Arthur Fitt (10)   120
Gaia Orecchia (7)   121
Nancy Hills (8)   122
Emilie Greene (10)   123
Flo Aguado (10)   124
Harry Dicker (8)   125
Isobel Harrex-Perks (8)   126
Harriet Brunton (10)   127
Lillie Packham (10)   128

St Peter's Catholic Primary School, Bartley Green

Frankie Brookes (10)	129
Connie Mcintosh (8)	130
Mitchell Nwokolo (9)	132
Aldrin Diljo (9)	133
Jorgie Bullock (9)	134
Meika Ivy-Georgia Foote (9)	135
Maisie Bullock (9)	136
Archie Strange (9)	137
Eva Beale (9)	138
Alfie Boffey (9)	139

The Herne Junior School, Petersfield

Anna Rocher (10)	140
Milo De Giovanni (10)	142
Barney Bryant (10)	144
Chloe Williams (10)	146
Leela Sheridan-Maan (10)	148
Megan Llewelyn-Williams (10)	149

Wyborne Primary School, New Eltham

Aiko Wilkoszewska (9)	150
Lottie Franklin (10)	151
Danielle Tinnion (10)	152
Taysia Weston-Lawson (9)	153

Ysgol Gynradd Gymraeg Caerffili, Caerphilly

Jessica Clements	154
Molly Jones (9)	156
Alessandra Winter	158
Tyra-Jae Taylor	160

The Diaries

The Incredible Diary Of A Super-Duper Mega Dog!

Dear Diary,

Today was a *big* day. Let me tell you about it... So, me and Tommy (my superhero owner) were taking a walk when the *evil* Dr Diabolical and his pet, Whiskers the cat, suddenly snatched Tommy! "Mwahahaha!" laughed Dr D.

I used my powers to fly up, but he had already flown away. I whined for a few hours until I realised I could fly. *Silly me*, I thought, so I flew to his not-so-secret base. It is in the middle of the city. I mean, honestly! So, first I created a clone of myself to trick the guards. Believe it or not, it *worked.* After I snuck in, I went through the door that said 'Do not enter, no villain in here'. *This guy is so smart*, I thought sarcastically. There he was! Somehow, Tommy escaped and Dr D wasn't here... Weird.

Pow! Before I could finish that thought, Whiskers came in through the roof. I assumed he was going to fight me, but instead he said, "I am so sorry for that. Dr D is a mean one. Would you like a lift home?"

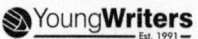

"Okay!" I said and, in the blink of an eye, we were back home. But now... I need a nap!
Signed,
Milo.

Tommy Brook-Johnson (10)
Akeley Wood Junior School, Wicken

Spooky Academy

Dear Diary,

This week has been like a roller-coaster ride. It's been good and bad. Monday was my very first day of Spooky Academy. I had to walk for thirty minutes (which felt like the longest thirty minutes of my life). As soon as I walked through the school gates, I heard roars of laughter. People were saying, "Why is she slimy and red?" When I heard them talking about me, I had to hold back a river of tears. After that, I lied, I said I was sick and stayed off until Wednesday.

On Thursday, I didn't listen but in my head I thought, *rude, I come here to learn I'm not a supermodel*. I got through the day and I'm now the top of my class. But I still felt depressed and isolated.

On Friday, a blue fluffy girl approached me with ten other people and talked to me nicely. I was astonished. We laughed and soon the whole school wanted to be my friend. I helped others with homework and now I was seen as normal. I had a sleepover with Kayla, Chelsea and Sophie. I did a few cheeky dabs and we stayed up till 4am. It was so fun.

Sophia Knowles (9)
Capenhurst CE Primary School, Capenhurst

The Diary Of A Library Book

An extract

Dear Diary,

I've had such a topsy-turvy day! I was just chilling with my friends on this very tall shelf-looking thingy, chatting about the animal book section, when my friend got picked up by this hu... man? I was very mad! He left me (I thought he was my friend)!

A few days later, everyone had left. The random book section, the animal book section, the food book section; they all left me. It felt like a party only I wasn't invited to... After that, I got so bored that I fell asleep. When I woke up from my nap (it felt really good), there was a young human standing at my face (her green top was beautiful) then she picked me up and walked over to this other human and they were so loud (I hoped they knew that it was a library, not a fish market)! At her square thing with a triangle on top, with a rectangle with a circle on and another four squares on it... I think humans call it a house? Anyway, we went in and sat on this fluffy thing. Well, *she* sat on it, not me. Then she started to read me! She was pulling on my pages (I did

not like that)! Let's just say... I gave her a paper cut... I like revenge! After that, she put me down on the fluffy thing and left. I think she had learnt her lesson!
A few hours later, she grabbed me again...!

Abigail Culbert (9)
Capenhurst CE Primary School, Capenhurst

An Adventure With A Dragon

An extract

Dear Diary,
You won't believe the past twenty-four hours I've had. It all started when I was sitting on my iPad. A couple of minutes later, my mum came in and told me I had to turn it off and go to bed. As I lay in bed and closed my eyes, I dreamt I was riding a dragon in the moonlit sky. Then, all of a sudden, I was awoken by the loud sound of footsteps on my roof. I went up to investigate when, all of a sudden, out of nowhere stepped a creature I only ever thought existed in fairy tales. It was a dragon. I started to back away, I was absolutely terrified. It was until he spoke that I stopped trembling. These were his words:
"Hello, I think I'm lost."
I replied in a sweet voice, "I'll try my best to help you." Then, suddenly, he had swooped me up and I was riding on his back in the star-lit sky. He took me to a place called the Enchanted Forest where we had hours and hours of fun. Then, without even thinking about it, another dragon not too similar to him popped out of the bushes and started attacking my dragon. He was fighting for mine and

his lives. Then the other dragon unexpectedly grabbed a sword out of nowhere and started to really injure him. He fainted and started to run out of air. The other dragon cackled almost wickedly...

E N (9)
Capenhurst CE Primary School, Capenhurst

The Diary Of A Tree

Dear Diary,
Today has been an unusual day.
I was looking over all of the other trees standing below me, wondering if something or someone would pass by. I was staring at the pond next to me when a creature's reflection appeared. It wasn't just any creature, it was a human (exciting!). It came over and leaned on me, reading a book (not so exciting), so I went back to staring at the trees. A few minutes later, I felt something tickling my trunk. It was the human climbing on me! She went and sat on one of my branches before she climbed to another. Now we could both look over the horizon of trees.
Sadly, she went home but about ten minutes later she came back with some pebbles. She took her shoes off and dipped her feet in and they threw some pebbles in the pond. After a while, she took her feet out and climbed my trunk (again). When she got to the top, she plucked an apple off me and sat down, happily smiling as the glorious

peach sunset drifted down. We sat there for a while before she hugged my trunk and said goodbye.
I hope I'll write again soon.

Sophie Osborne (9)
Capenhurst CE Primary School, Capenhurst

The Diary Of A New Pet

Dear Diary,
What a journey I've had today. After all the drama of being out in the cold, I was finally taken to a shelter. But I'm the only dog here. Well, at least I thought I was, until I met Prince. He was really nice to me, then Prince was adopted and I was alone and all sad. At least they took care of me. Until this one girl and boy came, I didn't know what was going on when a carer came to pick me up in a crate, and put blankets and toys inside with me and locked the blue crate. The man handed me to the girl with long brown hair and ripped jeans on. They both looked really sweet.
Later that day, I arrived at a random house. It was beautiful. They took me into this room just for me and they trained me and now they're my new family. They named me Teddy and I go on walks every day and I even see my best friend, Prince. We play together on the field right beside my house and now I'm the happiest dog in the entire world. I love my family and my friend, Prince.

Heidi-Rose Warmer (9)
Capenhurst CE Primary School, Capenhurst

Taken Away

Dear Diary,
At first, I lived a happy life but one day two people took me away. But let's start from the beginning.
I was playing with my eight sisters and seven brothers and my owner. She said that someone was going with a new owner. I didn't want to leave my home, so I hid under the table with my special squeaky toy. Then I found my really, really, really special toy. I got it when I was born. Then I heard a knock on the door. I hid myself, then my owner picked me up by my fuzzy fur! Well, luckily for me, I still had my really, really, really special toy with me. I remembered about my other siblings! I forgot to say goodbye. Soon, I was in a *car!* I tried to jump out of the window, it was locked. Then a boy got in. I felt scared. Then, when I was in the 'home', I had to stay upstairs, then I heard someone come in. I tried to run downstairs, but the boy jumped on me. He turned the football on, then two kids came in. They cuddled me.
Bye!

Bella Ward (8)
Capenhurst CE Primary School, Capenhurst

The Diary Of A Hamster

Dear Diary,
I have had an extraordinary day. So, I live in this house with these four people and these things they call pets. And every second of my life, they try to kill me. Today, I fell over and then I hit myself in the face (I didn't like it) and they started laughing (I didn't like it again). So, I started chewing at the cage and ran away.
I found this place, I think it is a leaf place. I found a tree, so I started climbing it and decided to relax. I heard some rustling in the green stuff. But I leaned forward too much, then suddenly I started falling. But I thought, *I can fly, I can fly*, and I thought about it so hard I did it! I was flying. Woah! I decided I was gonna fly to this thing called a park. I went to the place and saw my four people running around, holding a lost hamster picture of me. Then a girl, I think called Charlotte, picked me up and we went home. And nobody was mean again.
See you tomorrow.

Charlotte Rowson (8)
Capenhurst CE Primary School, Capenhurst

A Stationary Life

Dear Diary,

Once, I was sitting in a pencil case, waiting to be used, when I thought about this thing that happened and I didn't want it to happen again. So, I got my friends to listen, like Rubber and Pencil and Gluestick. I said to them, "Once, I was in a pencil case on the 18th of April and I definitely remember. So, while I was lying in there with Glue, Pen, Pencil and Ruler, I was waiting to be picked. I saw a person. When he sat down, I was so happy like my friends. I heard a noise, the pencil case opened, he was going for me! But then he went to the pen and it closed again."

Then the teacher said, "No art today." I was like *no!* But then I thought. I could still be used in maths. It was maths, my only chance to be used and, no! He got Pencil and Glue and Rubber and not me. I was so sad, so I went to lie down and sleep. And that's the end. I will write again soon.

Riley Fisher (9)
Capenhurst CE Primary School, Capenhurst

A New Life As A Butterfly

Dear Diary,
I've had a sad and happy day.
So, first of all, I'm a caterpillar. Yes, that's right, a caterpillar. But all my friends are butterflies, so, yes, they can all fly and I can't, so that makes me sad. My friends try and help me, but they just say, "Eat more leaves and get fat." Yes, but I just think that's rude. So, I tried it and, yes, I got *verry*... fat! I went to my friends and said, "What do you think? This is fatness!" Yes, I got mad. When it was night, I slept on a low tree branch about 5cm long. Goodnight... *Zzzz*.
The next morning, I woke up in an orange cocoon! So, I bit a hole in the cocoon and got out, and... I'm a butterfly! So, I swooped into the air, singing... "I'm a butterfly, dodododo." I was so happy to fly with my friends, and that was my day.
Hope I write to you tomorrow.

Melia Burkey (8)
Capenhurst CE Primary School, Capenhurst

The Life Of A Clumsy Colour

Dear Diary,

Today, I was playing with my friends (I am Cyan, by the way!), then I decided to find something to eat. I was passing by the Ferris wheel in an odd world and I tripped over a box! Talk about clumsy! I was stuck, obviously, because I don't have arms. It was *sooo* embarrassing! And I stared at the box and tried not to cry, I couldn't help it! I asked myself, "Why am I so clumsy?" A boy in the distance came up to me. Was it a cookie? Blue? A normal man? No, it was Yellow, my best friend!

"Why are you sad, Cyan?" he asked.

"Because I tripped," I replied.

"I'll help you up, Cyan," he said.

"Thank you!" I cried.

"My pleasure!" he shouted. I ran back to my home and thought about doing something nice for him. Anyway, I'll write soon.

Bye for now, Diary.

April Wells (8)
Capenhurst CE Primary School, Capenhurst

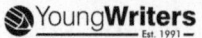

My Day As A Turtle

Dear Diary,
I was lying in the golden sand this afternoon and somebody came and picked me up. I was very angry. If you didn't know, I am a little emerald-green turtle.
Sorry. About the girl who picked me up. At least, I think it was a girl who picked me up. Guess what? They used me as a princess in a sandcastle! At least they made a moat so I could be in the water. I was fuming, my head was about to blow up.
By the way, my name is Charlotte Rose Champion. You might be like, what, a turtle named Charlotte? My mum gave me that name.
Back to the girl who put me in a sandcastle. I tried to wriggle away, but my legs are too stumpy and small, so I didn't move anywhere. By the way, my best friend is Ruemu, she's a squid. She is the bestest friend in the world.
That's it for today. I will write again tomorrow. Bye-bye.

Emily Fereday (8)
Capenhurst CE Primary School, Capenhurst

Life On A Kitchen Table

Dear Diary,
I was in the bottom of a pot. I was looking for something to do, there was nothing to do. Then I got scared. I was moving! I did not know what to do, I was starting to get really, really, really worried. Then I met my friend, Mia.
"Hi."
She was making a potion, I did not know what, but it was pretty fun to listen to her. Then, *poof!* There was smoke. It stank, then there was... a gigantic bang. Then I could see light. I didn't know, maybe it was a miracle. I was a bit wet (that felt uncomfortable). Let's carry on, shall we? Then I do not know what did it, but I was happy. I got dried (that made me happy). I was in something called 'a house'. Does not matter about that. I was in a kitchen, on a table.
Sorry, that's all I've got for ya. See you next time.

Mia Rose (8)
Capenhurst CE Primary School, Capenhurst

A Day In The Life Of A Football

Dear Diary,

Yesterday, I was fuming and you won't believe what happened... I was minding my own business with my circular friends and, suddenly, I was kicked from behind (*owww!*). That really hurt. Then, for some reason, loads of people came on the grass with me. I was confused. Why were so many people coming on the grass? A whistle blew and some people started kicking me. Someone kicked me that hard, I massacred across the grass, into a net. People started celebrating! That hurt my ears. It got worse!

At the end of people kicking and throwing, some person roughly picked me up and put me in their car! And then, when I got out of that smelly car, that person dragged me into a shop. It was Sports Direct! I got left there! Am I gonna get another owner?

I will write again soon.

William Riley (8)
Capenhurst CE Primary School, Capenhurst

Life's A Ball

Dear Diary,
Today has been awful and here's what happened...
I was relaxing in my tube, then I got pulled out, so I shouted, *"Aliens!"* Then he squeezed me, prodded me and threw me to the ground (talk about rude). After that, the thing grabbed a stick with a net and hit me! I thought in my head, *is this my life now?* and another hit me and it went back and forth (my bum was getting bruised). Then I hit the ground, so I screamed, *"Aarrgghh!"*
"What was that?" said the thing. Then someone picked me up and took me somewhere... I checked and I was at the used ball centre!
I will write again soon.

Fletcher Swift (9)
Capenhurst CE Primary School, Capenhurst

The Wannabe Rock Star Princess

Dear Diary,

You will never believe what happened today!

Well, I was in my bed, looking at my guitar and wondering why I couldn't be a rock star princess. My mum thinks that I should be an elegant princess and I should grow up to be like her.

When it was dinner, I thought that I should tell her that I wanted to be a rock star, but when she said no, she said it so loud that she blew me off my chair!

After dinner, I was weeping in my bedroom when I saw a light on my guitar peg. I walked towards it, then a voice said, "Follow your dreams." I talked to my mum and that's how I became the rock star princess.

Ruemu Edewor (8)
Capenhurst CE Primary School, Capenhurst

I Get By With A Little Help From My Friends

Dear Diary,

Today has been a weird day. First, I got abandoned! I didn't know where to go. But, luckily, I found a friend. At first, I thought I was going to eat it, but we became friends. So, we went for a walk. It was wonderful. Until a cat came! I thought, *I am only a kitten.* I screamed!

He said, "Who are you and what are you doing here?"

I said, "Oh, sorry, I was just trying to find a place to stay."

He said, "Okay, I can help you." He walked me to a place I could stay. He was amazing. I hugged him. Yes!

Orla Baxter (7)
Capenhurst CE Primary School, Capenhurst

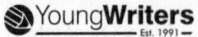

A Painful Day

Dear Diary,
I have had a roller coaster of a day. I was in a field and some white creature was coming towards me. It pinched me and took me to a mysterious place and was tying me to its person. He launched me to the wall and kept on pinching me. They're dead rude, right? This creature was taking me somewhere soaking. Oh no, not in the puddle. Oh, I was dirty now. I was fuming. Finally, they dropped me and I was covered in bruises. You were done... Oh no, you were hitting me.
Yes, I flew out the window. And I'm in a tree. I am glad that's over.

Flynn Phillips (8)
Capenhurst CE Primary School, Capenhurst

Being A Squishmallow

Dear Diary,

You will never believe what happened a week ago. I was sitting on a shelf with my Squishmallow friends, minding my own business, doing the totally 100% right thing. Then, from out of nowhere, I was poked, squished hugged and kissed. Oh, talk about disgusting. This was way worse... I was carried all the way to this thing they call a register, they scanned me on a bright red light and then they threw me into a very uncomfortable bag, so uncomfortable. Talk about rude.

I'm just an innocent little frog... *Prrrr...*

Sophia Morris (9)
Capenhurst CE Primary School, Capenhurst

Being Kicked Around

Dear Diary,

I have had the most painful day! It all started when I was being picked up by a giant thing with a fluffy thing on top of its head. Then I felt something prickly on my bottom, it was a shoe but not just a shoe, it was a spiky shoe! Suddenly, I was being kicked in a net and it knotted me up. My ears, that you cannot see, were hurting so I had to cover them because lots of these giants were shouting because a team, I think called Everton, won a game. But I did not find any games. After all that, I was fuming!

Verity Cottrell
Capenhurst CE Primary School, Capenhurst

The Life Of A Football

Dear Diary,

I was sitting in a goal, but then the most powerful kick hit me and I went across the green pitch. It hurt, then I got kicked again and then people started screaming and people were also sad. I felt bad, but that did not stop the hurt. I felt sad, lonely and depressed. Then I heard a whistle. People looked so excited, but the players on the other side looked sad.

They took me home, it felt so much better. I hope that doesn't happen again.

I will write again.

Euan Metcalfe (9)
Capenhurst CE Primary School, Capenhurst

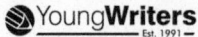

The Pro Golf Ball

Dear Diary,
I felt so nervous sitting on this tee. I didn't know what was going to happen. Suddenly, *bang!* I got smashed. I got hit at least 300 yards. Then I landed on the green, rolling towards the hole. Then, a hole-in-one! This happened at Sawgrass Golf Course. I was feeling hurt, lonely and upset. Suddenly, a big hand picked me up and kissed me.
Now I am a champion. I feel great.

Mitchell Brown (9)
Capenhurst CE Primary School, Capenhurst

The Life Of A Tree For Me

Dear Diary,

I've had a weird day!

I was in my house and, suddenly, me and my friends started to fall. I was terrified of hurting myself when I hit the floor. To my surprise, I was fading brown! And my home did not have anyone in it. Instead, me and my friends were on the floor and *really* brown! I was no longer my emerald-green tree, I was a boring, brown, twiggy tree.

Nora Connor (8)
Capenhurst CE Primary School, Capenhurst

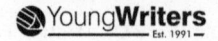

What Is Afoot?

Dear Diary,
I have had the worst day ever.
First of all, it started great. I was lying in my cushioned home until someone put me on their stinky feet. I was furious, I even passed out. But I stayed strong. After, I fought the awful stench. I was used to kick a ball into a net.
I'm tired, so I think I might go to bed.
Bye.

Finley Franks (8)
Capenhurst CE Primary School, Capenhurst

My Diary

Dear Diary,
I was happily minding my own business and then Jim grabbed me and slapped me against Anjy. I was disgusted at how Jim treated me! He did it like five times, over and over. Then Anjy landed on the grass, she was bruised all over but she was okay. Let's see what happens next...

Penelope Smith Lum Wai (8)
Capenhurst CE Primary School, Capenhurst

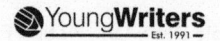

Performance Gone Wrong

Dear Diary,
On Monday, I was at Luke's Oil Stadium and then it was my turn to perform.
I hit backflip, I b-r-o-k-e!
I had to get dragged off by the dirt squad...

Seb Dunbar (8)
Capenhurst CE Primary School, Capenhurst

Day 37

Dear Diary,

It's day 37 in the secret passage. We are still trying to hide. But outside in the horrible world is war. We can't get much sleep as day by day, night by night, there is screaming, bombs going off and... death. You can tell when there is death, for you hear a poor soul stop screaming. It feels like the world is ending. We barely have any food and when people kindly bring us food we need to split it for all of us. I usually give half of mine to Holly, my four-year-old sister. I can't even describe what I have been through. Mother has been killed and Father badly injured. I love my home, but we have to flee.
All I ever know was bombed. My room. My bed. My *family*. All my memories... *Gone.* It is my birthday tomorrow, but it won't be the same with the war. Mother dead, Father can't walk. We don't know if our cat made it and, oh no, they're here. With guns. Oh no...

Tilly Hird (9)
Cotgrave Candleby Lane School, Cotgrave

A Wickedly Whimiscal Misadventure

Dear Diary,

Today was unlike any other! Oh, the chaos and the unexpected turns that unfolded. Truly a day to remember!

It all started with a mysterious artefact that managed to travel into my possession. Out of complete temptation, with Sarah and Mary by my side, oh, Dear Diary, don't you worry, the Sanderson Sisters are back in Salem, ready to experiment! But little did we know this *thing* had a mind of its own! Suddenly, we found ourselves in a paranormal dimension! Everything was topsy-turvy. People were dressed as witches but not the wicked kind like us. They celebrated Halloween with enthusiasm, unaware of the real magic lurking among them. The world was playful... Wait, is this *Crucible Hollow?!*

Yours wickedly,
Winnie Sanderson.

Freya Shread (8)
Cotgrave Candleby Lane School, Cotgrave

An Army That Will Return

Dear Diary,

It is another threatening day where I will hide secretly in my basement. My family and I haven't eaten in days. I heard loud bangs outside while my family were huddled up. I walked over to the door that leads out to our house and out of the basement. However, before I knew it bombs went off under my feet. I could feel the ground shaking as I heard voices breaking into our house. People were knocking down every single brick. I was terrified. I ran to my family, standing at the back wall. Suddenly I heard the army coming closer, rumbling through our precious memories. Then somebody or something entered and was coming closer to us...

Grace Nickerson (9)
Cotgrave Candleby Lane School, Cotgrave

Izzy, The Superhero

Dear Diary,

Izzy woke up and got her cape on, ready for the day. She ate her breakfast, she went to the park, someone was riding their bike and, oh no! They fell over. When they fell off their bike, Izzy flew up and then down to pick them up. Everyone started to clap and clap and clap. Izzy gave the girl called Eva a sticker. Izzy then decided to go to the zoo because she wanted to see her favourite animal, an elephant. It had hurt its leg because it slipped over its water in the zoo. Izzy went to the cage and put a plaster on Elephant's right leg because that was the leg that got hurt. That's Izzy's day. To be continued...

Eva Nembhard-Perry (8)
Cotgrave Candleby Lane School, Cotgrave

My Peer Pressure Necessity

Dear Diary,

Today at school my friends said that they would go to South Wolds but my other friends want to go to South Notts for Year 7. I honestly don't know what to do. Do you have any ideas?

I personally love being with my friends but when I have to pick sides, that love turns to hate as they know I hate sides. Plus, the thought of having some friends but not them tears me to bits.

Guys, I've made my decision and... I'm not going to South Wolds, which leaves me to tell you that I'm not going to South Notts either. I am going to... Toot Hill! This will be a chance to make new friends!

Josephine Grant (9)
Cotgrave Candleby Lane School, Cotgrave

Dinosaur Shredder

Dear Diary,

Today I heard on the news a dinosaur fossil that had been discovered underwater was to be dug up. After the world changed they would have been buried in water. That's why archaeologists thought they might be fossils underwater so I snuck to their top-secret HQ where the mission was to be launched. What I did is hid their diving suits and went with them.

The craziest thing happened after they dug for two minutes. A live dinosaur/T-rex jumped out and shredded the archaeologist so I quickly snuck away.

Lily Skipp (8)
Cotgrave Candleby Lane School, Cotgrave

About School

Dear Diary,

Today I went to school and when I was at school my teacher pronounced that we were going to a Year 6 play and the play was to start at 9:15. I was very excited to see the Year 6 play. The play was called 'I'm An 11-year-old, Get Me Out Of Here'. It was in the lunch hall. The play was funny and lovely. After the play, we went outside for 15 minutes. Next, my teacher pronounced and explained this sheet. We didn't finish our diary entries then so in the afternoon we finished. When we were in the lunch hall my lunch was rice, corn and taco. I loved my lunch and I got to finish my diary.

Amy Hoang (7)
Deptford Park Primary School, Deptford

A Trip To Nigeria

Dear Diary,

You will not believe what happened yesterday! My mum treated me to a trip to Nigeria. I also nearly learned all of the words for 7-year-olds. My brother also came on the trip. I met people and they were so nice that they became my friends. We went to the Nigeria store and it had a lot more than London's store. So because its store had so much stuff we decided to buy some. My brother met people named Leo and Samuel, they were super nice to him.

Samuel Faux (7)
Deptford Park Primary School, Deptford

Family Day Out

Dear Diary,

Last week, on Saturday, I went to the park with my family and my dad pushed me so high. I was so terrified and screamed but I had fun! After, I went on the slide and slid down, it was fun. Then it was time to go home and I was not happy because I wanted to go on the spinning twirl. When we got home me and Ava played in our room and then we had dinner, which was chicken and rice. I put sweet chilli sauce on mine and it was scrumptiously yum!

Aniyah D'Aguiar (7)
Deptford Park Primary School, Deptford

My Fun Day

Dear Diary,

Yesterday I went on my dad's iPad and I did my mathematics. When I logged in I went on 'guest' and did all of them then I went on Busy Things and did English. I made snowflakes. I won every single race and I got one hundred and sixteen coins. Then it was dinner time and I had the red-hot chicken that my mum bought with rice. When I was eating I watched Minions: The Rise of Gru. After I rested my belly I had a doughnut.

Kiro Osei-Poku Boakye (7)
Deptford Park Primary School, Deptford

A Rabbit That Was Very Furry

Dear Diary,
I have a rabbit that is very cute and it is white and I have three names for my rabbit. My favourite teachers are Safiya, Jenifer and Donna, they are my favourite teachers. That's why I love school and my favourite subjects are maths and science. I have six friends and was in the blue team for sports day. I love doing maths because it is fun and I like writing a little bit.

Mahsheed Hurmat (8)
Deptford Park Primary School, Deptford

Scaredy-Cat Mum

Dear Diary,

Last Sunday I went to my cousin's house for her birthday party. She's six but still shorter than me. We had some delicious chocolate cake. After that, we went to the London cable car and my mum screamed like a girl. I said, "Mum, you are a scaredy-cat!" and she laughed. It was a good day!

Nour Guendeba (7)
Deptford Park Primary School, Deptford

The Dance Winner

Dear Diary,
I was at school where there was a dance competition. I wore my best dress and shoes. The dance competition was in the hall. All the parents came. I was happy to see my mum, dad, grandma and grandpa. I got on the stage and danced to a pop song. Everyone clapped and then the judge told me I was the winner.

Anaiah Kasangu (7)
Deptford Park Primary School, Deptford

At The Cinema

Dear Diary,

Last week, when I was at the cinema, I watched Sharkboy and Lavagirl. The villain boy was trying to stop Sharkboy and Lavagirl. They were using their powers to stop the villain boy. I was so happy and very excited when they stopped the villain and it was on the news!

Jashaun Taylor (6)
Deptford Park Primary School, Deptford

My Surprise Computer

First, you won't believe my dad. He bought me my own computer and it has my mum's account and it has my sister's password. After that, I asked my mum when my baby sister would come? She said 2023!
The baby came on January 27th 2023! I was so excited. Best day ever.

Alexis Afrane-Ankama (7)
Deptford Park Primary School, Deptford

The Naughty Cat, Salem

Dear Diary,

My cat climbed up and he broke the mirror and me and my mum thought it was my brother or my sister. Our cat, Salem, ran up on the cupboard and broke the mirror. He ran upstairs and hid under my bed. He is sooo naughty and I was so shocked!

Skylar White (6)
Deptford Park Primary School, Deptford

At Greenwich Park

Dear Diary,

I went to Greenwich Park. On the way, me and my brother were playing rock, paper, scissors. So when we were there we got out of the car. Me and my brother played hide-and-seek and I was the seeker. I was happy and I found my brother.

Isaac Fernandes (6)
Deptford Park Primary School, Deptford

Sparkly Doll

Dear Diary,

Yesterday, on Monday 12th July 2023, I wanted a special doll. It was my birthday and on my birthday, on my bed, I saw a doll. The doll I really wanted! I was very excited and happy. It was very sparkly so I called it Sparkly.

Israel-L Sarpong (7)
Deptford Park Primary School, Deptford

Eason's Grandad's Birthday

Dear Diary,

Yesterday I went to meet my grandad because it was his birthday and it was so fun! It was the first time I had met my grandad. He looked old! He was fun and I now hope to go back to China and see him again soon.

Eason Chen (7)
Deptford Park Primary School, Deptford

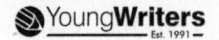

It Made My Day!

Dear Diary,

Yesterday I went to the beach and I threw some rocks then I took some home. After, I went home and when it was bedtime I had a smile on my face. I was excited. I hope my cat doesn't eat the rocks!

Maria Benzadi (7)
Deptford Park Primary School, Deptford

My Day At The Beach

Dear Diary,

I went to the beach today to have a swim and play in the sand then I had a picnic. My grandma played in the sea with me. We picked up some rocks out of the sea. I felt so happy!

Emily Huang (6)
Deptford Park Primary School, Deptford

Is It Real?

Dear Diary,

I went to the theatre last Saturday and I saw a shark in the movie. I felt scared so I put my hands on my face because the shark looked real. It was so scary!

Jenny Tran (6)
Deptford Park Primary School, Deptford

My Best Prize

Dear Diary,
I went to Disney World and I rode on a roller coaster. I was so happy and surprised because I didn't know I was going there.

Nelvin Afriyie (6)
Deptford Park Primary School, Deptford

William The Wembley Boy

27th May 2023

Dear Diary,

I woke up early in my soft, fluffy bed. It was a special day. Me and my family were going to watch Luton vs Coventry in the play-off final at Wembley! I got dressed and we drove for a long time in a posh bus with my family all the way to London. We were singing some tunes loudly. As we arrived in London there were lots of fans singing as loudly as my brother (and he is loud!). We dropped off our bags at our hotel. Then we went into Wembley and had some delicious, mouth-watering food just before the game started. It was 15 minutes from kick-off and I was feeling nervous. When we got to our seats the stadium was as enormous as the Colosseum and as loud as 1,000 of my brothers combined! One half was as orange as the sun and the other was as blue as the sky. In the first half, about 30 minutes in, Luton scored and I was thrilled. All the Luton fans went crazy, it was epic. Coventry in the second half was the better team and eventually they scored, it was heartbreaking. After 10 minutes it ended 1-1. Then it was extra time and Luton scored, but it was handball. it went to penalties and the first 10

players scored and then Luton scored their 6th and Coventry missed! It was the best feeling ever going to Wembley and watching Luton win.
The best day ever!

Freddie Sheridon (8)
Hadley Learning Community - Primary Phase, Hadley

The Surprise Assembly

Dear Diary,

Today has been the best day ever! We just finished our reading test when the excitement began. It was 2:30 and we all thought we were in trouble because our lovely sweet teacher, Miss Taffinder shut the door and normally when she does that she has a serious chat with us. But this time she told us that she got a phone call saying that Mr Evans was holding an emergency assembly. I looked at Eva and she looked just as shocked as I did. Not to mention we would be picked up at 4:30 instead of the normal time. We lined up at the door and went. We all sat in a line and then the lights turned off. Then there were flashy coloured lights and I could not believe my eyes, it was my favourite singer, Ed Sheeran standing with his guitar. He sang us a couple of songs and we all sang. He signed our shirts and I even got to speak to him. Then it was home time and my mum and dad were thrilled!

Isla Pollard (8)
Hadley Learning Community - Primary Phase, Hadley

The Incredible Chocolate Factory Girls

I have a little book called 'The Chocolate Factory Girls'. Inside the glorious, beautiful book is beautiful looking words and of course pictures. Well, let's go to the book now. Well, I have a little teenage friend called Collie, oooh! I also forgot my name so, my name is Diana. Anyways, back to business... Well did you read earlier about my friend, her name is Collie, well we were having a fun, nice year and then we were separate. Well we were separate because we have been a little bit naughty for a week because we didn't want to play with each other so we didn't but then Collie wanted to play with me but I didn't so that's when we started the sad, disappointing fight and this is how we became friends again. So first we told the teacher because they're a teacher! Second, we just took a deep breath and said glorious words.

Lamar Hammami (8)
Hadley Learning Community - Primary Phase, Hadley

My Crazy Pony And Horse Adventure

Dear Diary,

Today I had a crazy journey so I was at a posh yard to pick up my long-awaited horse. His name is Blade and he is a flea-bitten grey, 15.3 hands, 6-year-old horse. He is drop-dead gorgeous! I quickly led him into the horse box and took him to the new yard but first I had to find his stable. Later on, I took him on a hack into our nearby jungle. At first, he spooked at a bird but he soon got over it. I thought he was in agony but he was pranking me. Soon after that, he spooked at something again but this creature wasn't a bird, it was a very mystical creature. It had a gold body and wings but it couldn't fly. It had pink and purple wings. As soon as I touched it I fell into a portal with horses and ponies inside but as soon as I did touch it I tried to walk away. This world was a horsey world. It had a posh, fancy barn and fancy dressage and jumping arena. I was having so much fun with Blade in the area but suddenly I got sucked back up into the portal and was back in the

new yard with Blade. I hugged him and then said bye to go and have my dinner at home.
That's my diary entry for the day. Bye!

Alesha Inskip (9)
Heathlands Primary School, Mansfield

The Zoo Catastrophe

Dear Diary,

My name is Reco, a parrot, and I am writing from a sad but happy place where I will not wish to tell you, you will have to find out. Now it was just yesterday when this happened. I was watching the terrific lion with anticipation while it was getting fed. You see the enormous wild lion loathes me and I have to be ready for it to strike. Just then a loud roar attacked my ears and as quick as a flash the lion broke out. A man who was working with the lion and was letting everyone out, as soon as I saw freedom I flew out to find a girl. Together we made a plan and made friends. I flew in the lion's cage because if the lion saw me it would go inside the cage to eat me and the lions, the leaders of the zoo, so the others would follow and go inside the cages too.

So, then it happened. *Nom, nom, nom!* The girl closed all the cages but the person who was letting everyone out is still at large. So I am writing from Heaven and hopefully everyone is happy... except the lion! The girl got a reward and she is happy too so the zoo is back to normal except there is no me!

Betty Allen (9)
Heathlands Primary School, Mansfield

Maisie The Detective

Dear Diary,
I was watching the news today and there was a story about the detective girl. It was insane and it went a bit like this... Maisie Hitchins watched Sherlock Holmes as a little girl, wanting to become the most ambitious detective in the world once she was older. But when she got into primary she got bullied for her determined behaviour of wanting to be a detective. People bullied her not just because of her dream job but about her hair as well. She had frizzy, bright and ginger hair. After her really bad life in primary it only got worse once she got into secondary school. She got told by kids and even teachers that she would never be able to reach her goals in life. Her parents told her that it was just a phase that she was going to pass and she'd want to get a better job such as a doctor or lawyer when she was older. She's so used to the behaviour of people that she doesn't even listen anymore.

Skye McCormack (9)
Heathlands Primary School, Mansfield

The Boy Whose Grandad Was A Hero

Dear Diary,

Today, as I was opening my father's daily newspaper to look at the football scores I saw something immaculate, there it was, I saw it right in the newspaper in front of me. I shouted my dad and he said, "Do you know that's your grandfather, he saved our town!"

I thought to myself, *I can go and have an adventure to find my grandfather,* so I set off. First I needed food so I got all of my life savings which was £5. I bought butter, bread, wine gums and I made my dad pay my allowance and got an extra £4 so I got two litre bottles of water.

I set off on my journey. I climbed the smallest mountain and the largest stairs until I got to block B, storey 3 and door 12. I knocked three times and there he was, the heroic, amazing, legendary man, my grandfather, who saved the prime minister from a house fire.

Freya Foster-Evans (9)
Heathlands Primary School, Mansfield

The Mario Madness

Dear Diary,

It was 9am when I woke up in Viral City. Me and Luigi were getting ready for our job. Then we ate breakfast and began our job at a rich house and we did plumbing then a vicious dog came and started to attack us so we hopped in a pipe to fix it then it broke and we went in a portal but my brother fell in the dark one and was gone. I went to a mushroom world when I fell down and a toad who was real helped me to a castle called Peach's Castle so I snuck in and told the queen to help me find Luigi and we had to do parkour to train and I did it. Then we went to a jungle and I turned and defeated Donkey Kong. Then we made our karts. I went for a fast one so we could find Luigi and we drove but Bowser was raging so we fought him and we teleported to Viral City and it was the end. Luigi was saved.

Corey Mitchell (9)
Heathlands Primary School, Mansfield

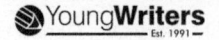

My Day In Paris

Dear Diary,
My name's Lily. I have a big family with two brothers and two sisters. It was a sunny morning yesterday, at 10am. We were walking in the fields. Happily we were thinking of going to eat and so we went to eat in a restaurant. My parents were there as well. We had food then we went to the shop. We bought some food and went home and it was very dark so we went to sleep.

Today my mum said we were going away. We went on an aeroplane. I said, "Where are we going, Mum?"

Mum told me we were going to Paris and I was so excited. In Paris I wanted something to eat so we went to eat a baguette and for dessert we had a croissant. We walked around all day then we went back home.

Odrija Baltina (8)
Heathlands Primary School, Mansfield

The School Day

Dear Diary,

My name is Kiara and today I've had a terrible day. Three bullies called Thomas, Joshua and Brendon bullied me! They started hitting me on the playground and blamed me for stealing their lunch money. They actually took my lunch money though. Next, in the lunch hall, when I was just about to sit down, they pulled my seat back and I tripped. After lunch, I told the teacher that they were bullying me and she tried to sort it out but just then, in the nick of time, they put their feet out and tripped me over! The teacher told them to go to the principal's office and they got told off!
I hope my school day will be better tomorrow but for now, bye.

Layla Inskip (9)
Heathlands Primary School, Mansfield

Amazing Fun Football

Dear Diary,

Yesterday, me and Dhilan went to the park in Rainworth to play football. When we set the goal up...

"I want to take shots," I said.

"How about we play hide-and-seek," Dhilan said.

"Okay," I replied.

"I'll hide first," said Dhilan.

"Okay," I replied. "I'll count to 30... 3, 2, 1, here I come!"

Once I had counted to 30 I had a look around the park but I couldn't find Dhilan anywhere.

"Oh no, I think I'm lost." Dhilan started to worry.

Luckily I found Dhilan and then we packed the goal up and went home.

Thomas Moss-Burton (9)
Heathlands Primary School, Mansfield

King Pickle's Journey To Hogwarts

Dear Diary,

I'm on an epic adventure to Hogwarts... I went to sleep and there was a mysterious banging noise at the window. I went to see it and it was a blue flying car with Ron Weasley inside. "Excuse me, what are you doing banging on my window at 6 o'clock in the morning?" I said.

"You're our new Harry Potter!"

Without another thought, he grabbed me and threw me in the back. This is all I can tell you because I'm still in the car!

Aidan Brasil Ibhanesebhor (8)
Heathlands Primary School, Mansfield

All About My School

Dear Diary,

I really like my school because it's fun. In school, we like doing lessons with a good teacher. My favourite subjects at school are maths, English, French, music, computing and art. My least favourite subjects at school are RE, history and geography.

Viktoria Lukasz (9)
Heathlands Primary School, Mansfield

Trip To The USA

Dear Diary,

I am here with good news. I know I've been away a month but the USA trip was great! I have so much to tell you I don't know where to start. I'll start with how I got there. I travelled using Doncaster Airlines, it was magnificent with all the massive landmarks. I'll name a few... like Mount Rushmore in South Dakota and I didn't forget my swimming shorts. We were in Utah after one hour to see The Great Salt Lake. It is located in the north of Utah. It is a physical feature, therefore, occurred naturally, it is like the sea though it is actually saltier than the sea. I went because I wanted to witness its salty atmosphere.

It was in the 1900s, to be exact, 1927, when the creation of Mount Rushmore started and ended in 1941. There are four former presidents' faces on it - George Washington, Thomas Jefferson, Abraham Lincoln and Theodore Roosevelt. All the heads are 18 metres tall.

I really enjoyed the visit but now I am on my way home from California. I want to visit the Hoover Dam and Niagra Falls next time I go.

Henley Smith (9)
Highwoods Academy, Mexborough

Trip To The USA

Dear Diary,

Don't I have a story for you! Excitedly I went on a trip to... the USA. Firstly, I witnessed fascinating landmarks. I will keep you updated, bye for now.

I went to go see The Great Salt Lake. The Great Salt Lake is natural therefore it is a physical feature. It is in Utah, in fact it's actually one of the largest lakes in USA. It contains salty water like the sea. It is however much more salty than the sea. I found out that you can float in the lake which I thought was very interesting.

As I explored USA I came across an enormous red bridge called the Golden Gate Bridge. This bridge is a mile long, in fact, it used to be the longest bright in the world. I was in shock when I actually saw it! By the time I'd walked across it, my legs were like jelly! I was exhausted. I must tell you about when I visited Hoover Dam, it is located on the border between the states of Nevada and Arizona. The dam is used to control floods for hydraulic power. It is 221 metres high and 379 metres long. Afterwards, I visited the Statue of Liberty, it is a large statue standing on a large island known as Liberty Island. The statue was a gift from the French people. She represents freedom and light, she is 46 metres tall.

Although I really enjoyed the wonderful visit and had a great time I had to return home. I hope I come back to visit the Colorado River and Mount Rushmore.

Kendall Goodyer (9)
Highwoods Academy, Mexborough

Trip To The USA

Dear Diary,
I couldn't believe I was in the USA, also known as the United States of America. Firstly, I caught sight of famous landmarks they were absolutely stunning. It was the most experience I've ever had I can't wait to tell you about it.

Firstly, I went to The Great Salt Lake which is located in the North of Utah. The Great Salt is a physical feature. A physical occurs naturally. Did you know the Rocky Mountains and the Great Salt Lake are located next to each other? Did you also know it is impossible to sink The Great Salt Lake? I loved The Great Salt Lake because I loved how beautiful it was.

The Space Needle is an observation tower located in the city of Seattle, Washington. Did you know that the Space Needle is a human feature which is manmade? When I saw the Space Needle I was flabbergasted by how towering tall it was. I was so delighted that I got to gaze at the Space Needle. I couldn't believe I could actually go inside it and it was even more amazing. Inside the Space Needle was even more enjoyable because it was beaming with light.

I amazingly enjoyed my trip to the USA and I hope to return in the future. If I do visit in the future I would like to visit the Hoover Dam and New York City.

Fareedah Hassan (9)
Highwoods Academy, Mexborough

Trip To The USA

Dear Diary,

You will never believe it but I had a wonderful trip to the USA. I witnessed nearly every famous landmark. I found them really interesting and I can't wait to tell you about all of the fascinating things I saw.

You wouldn't believe how many physical features I saw. My favourite was the Mojave Desert, it is one of four deserts located in the USA. It is in the South West, there is a valley there called Death Valley and the land actually sits lower than the level of the sea.

As soon as I saw the Golden Gate Bridge my jaw dropped. I was speechless for an hour after that. Me and my whole family gathered around and we took a beautiful picture in front of it with the sunset in the background. The year it was built was 1933 and I couldn't believe it was only one mile long, it looked about two miles long.

I really enjoyed my trip to the USA and I really didn't want to leave but I'm sure that in the future I will go back. I wish to see Niagara Falls when I do go back.

Lilly Hackford (9)
Highwoods Academy, Mexborough

Trip To The USA

Dear Diary,

I bet you will never believe me but I have travelled to The United States of America. Also, I laid my eyes on some mind-blowing landmarks! I can't wait to tell you what I recognised.

The Great Lakes are located at the border of the USA and Canada and since the border is a lake it's therefore a physical feature. Did you know that the Great Lakes are the fifth largest lake in North America? They also have a variety of wildlife. In my opinion, because I spotted so many animals and saw Canada from the USA.

Hoover Dam is located on the border between Nevada and Arizona. Did you know that the dam was constructed between 1930 and 1936, also it is used to control floods for hydraulic power. Fun fact: Hoover Dam is 221 metres high and 379 metres long. I flew over the Hoover Dam and trust me it was huge.

This trip was mindblowing and in the future, if I do come back, I want to visit Mount Rushmore and the Appalachian Mountains.

Vytis Karinauskas (9)
Highwoods Academy, Mexborough

Trip To The USA

Dear Diary,

You will never believe it but I have been on an incredible trip to the USA. I saw the Statue of Liberty and it was so big but I did not want to go inside it.

Also, I saw the Golden Gate Bridge and that was even larger and bigger than the Statue of Liberty. I saw a lot of people, cars and buses. It was so beautiful and I got to go on it because my dad parked his car on the Golden Gate Bridge. It is called the Golden Gate Bridge because they found a lot of gold there.

After I visited those places I visited the Grand Canyon which is in Arizona. It is famous and, it is 277 miles long. It has the Colorado River running through it. I went to see the view. I really enjoyed the trip but sadly I had to leave and go back home. I'm hoping to visit again to see the Golden Gate Bridge and the Colorado River again.

Lindsey-Rose (9)
Highwoods Academy, Mexborough

Trip To The USA

Dear Diary,

I bet you cannot guess where I have been. I have been on a trip to the USA on a plane over the Atlantic Ocean. I can't wait to tell you about the famous landmarks I saw.

When I went to the USA I went to the Grand Canyon. Did you know that the Grand Canyon is a mile deep and 277 miles long?

Excitedly I went to visit some famous landmarks that have been built by man. First of all, I visited the Statue of Liberty which stands tall on Liberty Island. It represents freedom and is 46 metres tall. It was built in 1886.

I really want to go back to the breathtaking USA but next time I'd love to adventure in The Great Salt Lake. Well, I cannot because you cannot go under the water. Well, I guess that is all from me, bye.

Jacob Rix (8)
Highwoods Academy, Mexborough

Trip To The USA

Dear Diary,

I should have told you that I've been on a trip to the USA! The first thing I viewed was The Great Salt Lake.

By the way, I went to The Great Salt Lake in Utah. It is a physical feature because lakes are made by rain. It is the largest lake in USA. It is much saltier than the sea. It put a smile on my face.

I expected that it would be much smaller but Mount Rushmore is way bigger. They began building it in 1927 and it was completed in 1941. It is in South Dakota and it's famous. Each carving is approximately 18 metres tall. There is a meeting room inside the doors.

I loved it and I wish I could go again. If I go back I will go to the Grand Canyon and the Golden Gate Bridge.

Mia Diggles (9)
Highwoods Academy, Mexborough

Trip To The USA

Dear Diary,
You will never guess what I did. I went to the USA. I laid eyes on famous landmarks.
I visited the Grand Canyon. It is located in Arizona. The Grand Canyon is a physical feature which occurs naturally. Did you know that the Grand Canyon is over a mile deep? The canyon made me speechless because it was amazing.
I visited the Statue of Liberty. The statue represents freedom. I went inside the Statue of Liberty and it was amazing. The statue is green and 46 metres tall. This amazing place is located on Liberty Island in New York.
I really enjoyed my trip, it was the best trip of my life and next time I would love to see Mount Rushmore.

Shillana Hibbins (9)
Highwoods Academy, Mexborough

Trip To The USA

Dear Diary,

You will never believe where Year 4 has been... We saw fantastic landmarks in the USA, it's a famous place and you can see everything there.

I visited the Grand Canyon. It is over 277 miles long and it's very good and the view is beautiful.

Then I visited the Golden Gate Bridge. It is a mile long. In the olden times there was gold found there.

I hope to return to the USA one day and see the Statue of Liberty and The Great Salt Lake.

Ryan Fisher (9)
Highwoods Academy, Mexborough

My Holiday

Dear Diary,

This morning, I woke up at 1:30am to catch the plane. It took three hours to get to Dundee Airport. I was the first one there. It was so fun because there was so much space. I waited for two hours to get on the plane. The plane ride was five hours to Spain from Scotland. The plane was so warm. When I got to my hotel it was nice, fancy, stylish, beautiful and peaceful. I unpacked immediately. I got my swimsuit on and jumped into the pool. I stayed in the pool for an hour. After that I went to a really super fancy and nice restaurant. I ate chicken nuggets and chips. Then I went back to the hotel and chilled on the nice balcony.
I can't wait till tomorrow.

Leah-Rose Wisniewska (9)
Seaton School, Aberdeen

My Trip To Australia

Dear Diary,
It is 2044 and I am looking for pieces to make my rocket sled.
I bought a rocket and metal rails. It took me two days to build the rocket sled. I was so excited to go to Australia. On the way, I saw Miss Russell running. Then I saw Australia. There were spaceships and space stations and people were jealous.
I said hello then they said hello so I went to their station to visit the Australian people. I ate some food. It was my favourite food. It was a sandwich with chicken and salami in it. I was so hungry.

Dear Diary,
It is now 2045.
I came back to Scotland and now I am writing this...

Piotr Bilinski (9)
Seaton School, Aberdeen

A Girl That Lost Her Dog

Dear Diary,

Yesterday I was giving my dog a walk then when we wanted to cross the road my dog started barking at a car for no reason. The person in the car got mad and just drove over my dog. It was able to escape but I was still sad about it. I was so mad and sad I cried all the way home. I was so tired. When I got home I told my mom and dad what happened. They were sad too.

Today I got a beautiful gift. It was a dog, a female dog. She was so beautiful. I cheered up. When it was time for breakfast I gave my mum and dad a hug for always being there for me.

Daniella Osakue (9)
Seaton School, Aberdeen

Me And My Friend

Dear Diary,

Yesterday was the best day ever! I went on an aeroplane and I flew to Florida. On the plane I had an ice cream for free and I got bubblegum flavour with syrup. The syrup was bubblegum as well! Next, I went to the beach and I saw my friend, Hot. On the beach it was beautiful and I saw a red fish in the sea! Then me and my friend, Hot, went to Disney World and we went on the Ferris wheel. Finally me and my friend climbed up a mountain. It took us an hour to climb the mountain and at the top of the mountain it was so pretty and we got a lollipop!

Nadia Mikulska (8)
Seaton School, Aberdeen

The Berry Line

Dear Diary,
Today I went to Berry City and went to the strawberry building, then suddenly a star shot out of the sky! Then Melody left the building and, *boom!* Something amazing happened. Melody quickly took a berry shield and then all her fans came and the star landed right next to Melody. Then she was on the news and she was screaming with excitement. Then she got the strawberry crown. She was the first person to ever get the star and the crown.

Nathan Bogdevic (8)
Seaton School, Aberdeen

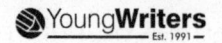

Going On Vacation With My BFF

Dear Diary,

Today was the best day ever! When I was taking a nap my best friend called me. I was shocked. She said I could go on vacation with her. She said, "Pack your bags now, we're leaving in an hour." So I packed my pyjamas, a teddy bear, a toothbrush and toothpaste. I said, "Can I have some lavender and blue shiny clothes?"

"Sure," she said then we went to the Rainbow Water Park. After, we slept, goodbye.

Zofia Uzar (8)
Seaton School, Aberdeen

Me And My Dog

Dear Diary,

Today I had a fun day with my dog, Cleo. This morning we went to Aberdeen beach and we played fetch. We played in the freezing cold water and I splashed Cleo. Then we went to Pizza Hut and got cheese pizza and ice cream. Next, we drove to Bennachie. It took an hour to get to the top and it was very cool. I could see everything from up high. Next, we went home and watched football together. Aberdeen won 2-0.

Orson Phillips (9)
Seaton School, Aberdeen

I Saved The World

Dear Diary,

Today I saved the world. This morning I was walking to work when I saw a supervillain called Hollie and she was robbing the shops. I flew above her and shot her with my Nerf blaster. She dropped the money and got out her funny blaster. I dodged all the shots she aimed at me. Someone called the police. The police came and arrested her. I got a medal and now I will get free food from the shops for life.

Ambyr Brown (8)
Seaton School, Aberdeen

Boti's Adventure

Dear Diary,

Yesterday it was very rainy. I was eating waffles for my breakfast when I heard sirens going nee naw! I saw the police break the door of the bank and heard them shout, "Put your hands up!" The police arrested the robbers and put them in the van. They took them to a maximum security prison for 100 years!

Boti Bokor (9)
Seaton School, Aberdeen

Best Day Ever

Dear Diary,

Today was a very fun day. My dad dropped me off at football and we won 10-0. I scored all 10 goals. I won a gold medal. After that, we climbed a high volcano. It took me an hour and 11 minutes to reach the top. After that, we went to the park. I played with Aoifa on the swings and I went so high.

Lily Allen (9)
Seaton School, Aberdeen

Best Friends

Dear Diary,

I had the best time ever because me and my bestest friend ever had a sleepover last night. We had so much fun. We played on the Xbox with his dog. His dog's name is Cosmo. He licked my toes and also nibbled my toes. It was so tickly that I laughed so hard and I almost died!

Jack Adams (9)
Seaton School, Aberdeen

Day In The Life Of Table 39
An extract

Dear Diary,
I am just a table. I should not get drawn on or get my head and table 40 slammed together. It all started with me getting all clean, polished down until class 1 came in, spilt water on me then Jessica came over and pushed me into table 38 then table 40 slammed into me. This was going too far, I was getting so annoyed. Then sadly the hall was occupied so they had to eat in the classroom. I had a peanut butter and jam sandwich all over me because they had a food fight when the teacher left for two seconds. I get more frustrated, more angry, and then boom, I heard was getting sat on by Leah, Myah and Ava and I started wiggling because I was getting unstable. Then they cleaned up and then I got flipped upside down because they needed to clean me. I was panicking. I could not breathe and they were spraying me with cold bubbly stuff. It was so cold and I was starting to stiffen up. My legs got tighter. Shortly after they wiped it off and then a new person walked in. She immediately got led to her seat and she sat to my table. She was so organised, we were a perfect match. As I calmed down she started swinging on

her chair and was kicking me until I fell over. I had had enough. I was putting so much weight on one side so they could not pick me up. I kept leaning and I gave up. I was getting too tired.

I don't think that I will ever be able to use my right side again. I had to count to tell to calm myself down...

Mylie Storey (11)
St Bede's RC Primary School, Denton Burn

The Pawsome Diary Of Jack The Cat

Dear Diary,

Yesterday I woke up. My owners were still asleep so I decided to be annoying and meow really loudly in their faces. When they woke up they fed me. I ate it all, obviously! Later on, I noticed them going to hang washing out, this was my moment! I decided to sneak out. Before I knew it I was in the jungle. I explored. *Oh a bird, I'm gonna get it!* I thought. I couldn't get it... Anyway, I kept exploring and exploring. The jungle felt like it went on forever. Something was grabbing me, *noooo! I must hide*, I thought. there was a cave, oh wait, it was just my owner's trampoline. Today I was in a daydreaming mood. After that, I needed a nap so I went into one of my many beds. Most of them I don't use but... anyway, so later when I woke up my owner was making her tea so I wanted the food. So I jumped onto the bench. Soon I was like a superhero on top of a building. It was a perfect place for a nap so I lay down until I rolled off... Yeah, that really hurt but what do humans say... Cats always land on their feet, so I did. I needed another nap... so I did! After a while, my owner was going to bed so they fed me again. I went to sleep dreaming about today's adventures.

Amelia Wansell (11)
St Bede's RC Primary School, Denton Burn

The Story Of Dotty The Dog

Dear Diary,

Today my mum took me on a walk with my little sister, Cherry, who is one year younger than me but she is also bigger than me. As we were on our walk Mum decided to let us off our leads and let us play fetch once we arrived at our destination which was a big field. But before Mum threw the ball she made us sit down and give her our paw so when we did what she asked. She finally threw the ball. As my sister is faster than me she always gets the ball but I still try to run and get the ball which is a lot of fun. I always run with my sister but as she was running she jumped over a log so I decided that I would give it a try since it didn't look that high. Then something bad happened. Once I jumped I tripped over the log and landed on my leg. So when I tried to stand up, I couldn't, I was in too much pain so my mum put my sister back on her lead then picked me up and carried me home. When we finally got home Mum put my sister away then she and Grandad drove me to the vet. After the nice man (the vet) did an x-ray on my leg he said I had broken it so he put a cast on me and put me in a wheelchair then I went home to have some rest.

Amelia-Lily Mott (11)
St Bede's RC Primary School, Denton Burn

Enzo's Bad Day

Dear Diary,

I am Enzo the black and tan ten-month-old long-haired German shepherd. My life is simple, not much to do, just a normal dog's life. But today was a bad day. It was a normal Saturday. I got up, had my breakfast, went on a walk, slept and slept and slept but then I woke up with so much energy and wanted to play then I went on my walk again and had my tea and went to bed or that's at least what my owners thought.

I was so happy that my real brother was seeing me tomorrow so I thought I wanted to do something naughty and cheeky. I decided to go and rip up a blanket, the ones my mum puts on the settee to stop me scratching it so I chewed it instead of scratching. I did it. I put a huge hole in the side of it, haha! Now I feel a bit guilty and I say sorry to the blanket, that's what you should always do but the blanket didn't even say 'thank you' or 'it's okay', I can't believe it! I feel nervous that my mum will find it. She will lock me outside in the garden, every dog's worst fear. I hate being locked in the garden.

Hannah Watson (11)
St Bede's RC Primary School, Denton Burn

The Survival Of The Fittest

Dear Diary,

The past two or three days I've lost all track of time... here is what happened.

The flight was going smoothly until I looked out of my window and saw something had caught fire. I was scared for my life and there was nothing we could do! A minute later the plane had nose-dived and we were only about 200 feet from the floor. Then we crashed and I'm probably one of the luckiest people in the world. I am the only survivor! Once I got up I barely could remember what happened until I looked behind me and it all came back. I looked around and the place looked familiar. I'd seen pictures of this place and I remembered why. It's one of the deadliest places on the planet... I was scared for my life. I couldn't move. I needed to find shelter but I ran into my first obstacle, it was a snake! I got past it easily though I just went the other way.

Today I found shelter so I'm okay for now...

Lewis Allen (11)
St Bede's RC Primary School, Denton Burn

How John Became A Hero

Dear Diary,

Yesterday was a good and bad day for me. I'm John, I've got two kids called Elliot and James and a wife. Today I got a call from NASA saying that a bunch of aliens raided NASA and kidnapped every worker. The man on the phone said, "Bring all of your squad from the RAF."

"Yes Sir."

I got all of my team and told them, "We need to go save everyone at NASA."

"Yes, Captain. Let's go."

When we got there I saw that NASA had been burnt to a crisp but everybody was outside safe and sound. Suddenly a green monster came and grabbed everyone so we zoomed past the monster and knocked him off his feet. He dropped everyone so we all opened the hatch and got in. Relieved we got everyone, we got the military to sort things out while we got everyone to safety.

Today we have been named heroes after saving the people.

Finley Wharton (11)
St Bede's RC Primary School, Denton Burn

The Diary Of Daisy

Dear Diary,
Today was fun, strange, exciting but mainly amazing. Sorry I haven't even introduced myself, my name is Daisy. I just turned 11 on the 8th of June. My favourite colour is pink, duhh, and today was my Year 6 leavers' trip and we went to the soft play. On the bus to the soft play I sat next to Amelia (my best friend). Once we arrived I was super happy and excited mainly for the ball pit. As soon as we entered the building me and Amelia ran straight towards the ball pit. We both jumped in at the exact same time and... I didn't stop, Amelia did but I didn't. I just kept on falling and falling until... I crashed but it was a soft landing. I looked around for a while and realised I was in a massive bouncy house! I looked up and saw in the far distance out popped Amelia's face. She saw me and came toppling down on top of me.

Libby Holden (11)
St Bede's RC Primary School, Denton Burn

A Day In The Life Of A Newcastle United Fan

Dear Diary,

You will not believe what happened at the Newcastle United stadium today! Here's what happened... The game started for Newcastle United, one game away from the Carabao Cup final. We knew we had to put in all our efforts in... Nottingham Forest were on the attack... What is this? Nick Pope ran out of his box and squandered the ball but it was a red card because it hit his hand... That means he will not be able to play in the Carabao Cup final. Dúbravka was subbed on for one of our players and the game continued. Some of the Newcastle United fans were leaving, knowing that he could not play in the final because he was loaned to Man United who we are playing in the final... We must rely on one keeper... Karius. We bought him from Liverpool and he is the only keeper we have. The game ended... We play Man United next...

Olly Wright (10)
St Bede's RC Primary School, Denton Burn

Diary Of Poppy The Lazy Cat

Dear Diary,

Today I woke up still knowing I'm a queen. So I trotted down the stairs and pestered my servant for food but I only got four Dreamies. I looked at my human with displeasure. So I angrily went into the living room then... a filthy mutt yapped so I hit her with my paw that was clean before it hit the mutt's face! Before long my human let me out so I went looking for food.

Eventually, I found chicken but Gingy was there so I quickly slapped him and ran away. I looked in other gardens to no avail so I sorrowfully meowed at my human's door. Eventually, I went back inside and upstairs. I looked at the hamster and hissed at her. Then I looked at the rodents before hopping onto the couch and sleeping.

Katie Howard (11)
St Bede's RC Primary School, Denton Burn

Dairy Of A Ukrainian Boy

Dear Diary,
I'm Ali and I come from Ukraine. My dad got me this diary to write all my adventures but this is how it all started. Wednesday 18th April 2022 was when I left my country. I was terrified. My house and my school were bombed, also it was not safe anywhere. So many people died; none of them did anything wrong. I grew up in a small home with my dad, my mum died when I was born. I don't really remember her nor miss her. I've got my dad and that's all that matters. I went on a long car trip to be safe with a comfy bed and food. I feel lucky to be here, no bombs and no screaming at night. It took ages to adjust in Romania. The language, weather and even the people.

Atefa Aymon Zamil (11)
St Bede's RC Primary School, Denton Burn

Doggy Day Out

Dear Diary,

Angel is my dog. She is a white Shar pei and today me and Angel went to the doggy park. We walked all the way to the doggy park. Angel jumped up on me. She was so excited. She ran into the big doggy park. She saw a black dog and she ran to it. Angel smelt her. They both ran around the tree. The dogs rolled on the grass and me and my friend stroked our dogs.

Me and my friend walked back home. When we got back home we had some food. My dog drank some water then I put my dog to bed and went upstairs and put on my pyjamas before going to bed.

Michael Tait (11)
St Bede's RC Primary School, Denton Burn

Harry Potter And The Cupboard

Dear Diary,

Today my aunt and uncle locked me in a cupboard. Every time Dudley comes down the stairs he stomps. The only time I'm allowed out is to eat or cook. I am basically a slave. I can't use magic beans. My wand is upstairs. I'm so sad I want to escape them. I'm so angry.

Paul Carling (11)
St Bede's RC Primary School, Denton Burn

When Bow The Dog First Met His New Family

Dear Diary,
Today I have been adopted into a lovely family. I've just started to get used to them, especially Chloe. She feeds me. She gives me treats. She strokes me and takes care of me. But there's a really annoying one called Jessica...

Jessica Nesbitt (11)
St Bede's RC Primary School, Denton Burn

The Incredible Diary Of Gem Island

Dear Diary,

I've been having the craziest couple of weeks of my life! I had breakfast with the whole family at a fancy restaurant. Then my brother stated that he was going on an adventure and wouldn't be back for a week or two. He bought a plane ticket with his money and set off. Time passed then I got really worried. I found out from my brother's friend that he had travelled to Gem Island. I brought a plane ticket with my money and flew to this island that I had never heard of before. On the way there we saw a silhouette of a dragon. Suddenly we saw the island then eventually landed on the mysterious place. I got off the plane and walked around for a bit. It didn't take long to see my brother lying on the floor. I checked his pulse and he wasn't alive. I saw the gigantic gates of the castle fly down. I stumbled in and caught sight of the gem. Then I ran to the glowing object, grabbed it and then I remembered my brother said it gives eternal life. I felt a change in my body. I instantly knew what to do with the gem. I ran outside and put the gem on my brother's lap then he opened his eyes and I said to him. "You're alive!" I told him

that I found the gem. I could see in his eyes that he was glad then we went back home and everything was normal.
Later that day I saw a newspaper article about me and my brother surviving Gem Island!

Ryan Smart (10)
St John The Baptist CE Primary School, Worthing

The Incredible Diary Of The Chicken Nuggets Vs The Ducks

Dear Diary,
Today has been a horrible, sad and happy day. I was taking a walk when I saw some ducks eating chicken nuggets. I rushed over and saw my best friend. Joe, one of the ducks was about to eat him. I sped over and grabbed my best friend and the other chicken nuggets. I ran whilst being chased by the ducks. I ran for what felt like hours, then I thought I'd lost them. I let the chicken nuggets run off. I talked with my best friend for a while then he took off. Suddenly it hit me, I had forgotten one of the chicken nuggets. I was so sad I had failed to save him. But then, you'll never believe it, I saw a McDonald's. I ran inside to see them eating chicken nuggets! I saw my parents being eaten. I ran away so fast while crying many tears. I couldn't believe it. So I ran back and started to fight the duck. I took a hard blow to the chest so I had to run. I went to find my best friend, he felt really sorry for me. I went to find my brother and told him what had happened. He was really sad. Then we went home and went to find our sister. We told her about what had happened to our parents. She cried for ages then I went back and

realised it wasn't our parents so I raced back to tell them the great news. My sister was so happy. My best friend felt happy for me and my brother said how happy he was.

Noah Cane (10)
St John The Baptist CE Primary School, Worthing

The Incredible Diary Of A Time Traveller

Dear Diary,

Today has been horrid. I woke up at the normal time of 6:10. Once I was up and dressed I trudged down the steep stairs. But then the worst thing imaginable happened... I slipped and my time machine broke. Next, I was sucked from 1891 to 1989! As I got slowly off the neatly paved floor I saw something odd... Lots of city folk. Looking down at some strange glowing triangular-shaped thing. I heard people talking. What's that strange thing in the sky? And why were they all wearing poppies? I pulled somebody over and asked. They simply gave me one and said, "WW2 and WW1." "What's that? And why did we have two world wars?"

I needed to get back. All of a sudden I saw a metal cruise liner. On the side it said: 'Find out the truth of the Victorian era'. That is where I needed to go as I clambered on with the sunset glistening on the

vast sea, changing the colour into a wonderful orange and yellow.
Dear Diary, it did not lead to the Victorian era but I am now in a museum.

Benjamin Hoadley (10)
St John The Baptist CE Primary School, Worthing

The Incredible Diary Of Parry Pencil

Dear Diary,

Today I escaped the vast jungle of toys known as Christopher's Preschool. But let's start from the beginning. I woke up today, picked up my bag, walked out of my cardboard hut and set off towards the jumble of a bookshelf where the ravenous children would eat their snacks and read (or rip) the books. Every night before the rushing waves of demented four-year-olds burst open the doors and trample the scraps below. All the stationary and toys go for a break in the adventure section on the ginormous shelf. Before I escaped I found an aeroplane rent shop for free! And the owner let me keep the plane (it was my lucky day). So I got on the plane and flew out the window, I've never been outside, it was beautiful! I only ever heard of trees, flowers, wind, civilisation, it was so amazing I could never escape its warm embrace... I lost control... I crashed! So now I'm chilling in the place of legends. The perfect place, a place of wind, of dignity, of fun... I'm in Christopher's Preschool playground!

Joshua Gordon (9)
St John The Baptist CE Primary School, Worthing

My Day At Disneyland

Dear Diary,

Today I went to Disneyland in a beautiful Beauty and the Beast dress which was gold and glittery. We went on some really fast and scary rides and met Disney characters all day. We went to have dinner in a Mickey Mouse restaurant and after we ate a massive plate of tasty food and we had a great surprise. Suddenly, all the Disney characters came out of a shiny door with a birthday cake. We ate it all up and then we went to a special room and I got my make-up and hair done by a princess who granted me a wish.

Next, we went to The Pirates of the Caribbean ship and suddenly Captain Hook swung in from the lookout on ropes and gave us a treasure chest filled with diamonds, gold, silver, bracelets, necklaces, earrings and free ride passes! And of course, a curtsey.

After all that excitement we went back to the hotel room because we were exhausted and I fell asleep instantly and dreamed of princesses and Minnie Mouse all night.

What a day!

Delilah Gordon (9)
St John The Baptist CE Primary School, Worthing

The Incredible Diary Of Annoyed Pencil

Dear Diary,
I need to tell you something urgent, and no it can't wait. I was, as usual, being chewed on by this snotty boy trying to do his homework. I honestly feel sorry for this boy's mum. I mean, first of all, they live in the smallest house in, well, get this, Mayhem Toilet Valley. Sorry, let me get back to the story... Well, second of all she works really hard to make this boy happy. That boy actually threw me into the bin. He must have gone a bit crazy... When the rubbish guy came and shouted to his co-worker, "I need a pencil to write down notes... I found one!" I wasn't sure why. After a few hours, we flew and yes, I was in a helicopter. Going to Buckingham Palace. When I realised what was going on, my blood ran cold. I was part of the biggest robbery! I didn't know what to do.
Right now I am in the corner of the glass holding the Crown Jewels writing this and I only have one thing to say... SOS!

Delilah Fitt (9)
St John The Baptist CE Primary School, Worthing

The Incredible Diary Of The Globe

Dear Diary,

Today has been so annoying because I was constantly being spun during a geography lesson. I thought I was about to vomit. The teacher was really mean to me, she kept on calling me names, like England, Mexico, New York, America and Brazil. I then got locked in a closet. As soon as the closet got unlocked by a teacher's little kid she threw me into a box that said 'Lost and Found'. I've heard so many stories about it by Ryan the Ruler. They were both right about the terrors in there. I found underwear, nappies and dried-out glue sticks. I made 'friends', they tried to use me to jump out of the box. I soon fell into a dream about me with Crookshanks from Harry Potter in a pet store where Hermione was his new owner. I soon 'woke up' and the Queen of Hearts was standing in front of me.

PS: I woke up for real because everything was a dream and I was still locked in the closet.

Mia Leaney (10)
St John The Baptist CE Primary School, Worthing

The Incredible Diary Of Rosie Rubber

Dear Diary,

What a crazy day I had! I woke up to find I was in a pencil case with my friends, Rachel Ruler, Peter Pen, Glenda Gluestick and Penny Pencil. I went to chat with my friends (all my friends) then the pencil case suddenly opened with light. I got grabbed by a boy and handled quite roughly to rub out a drawing. You will never believe what happened next. I was thrown to the corner of the teacher's desk. When suddenly a furry face with a twitching nose appeared from a hole. I didn't know what it was. After the teacher saw the furry face she screamed at the top of her lungs. She saw me and picked me up and asked the class who I belonged to. The boy (who had thrown me) claimed me. I was promptly chucked into the pencil case. I peeked out from a gap in the zip and I saw the teacher picking up the furry face and discovered it was a... mouse. I love mice! Anyways, that's the end of my crazy day. Bye!

Scarlett Ko (9)
St John The Baptist CE Primary School, Worthing

The Incredible Diary Of Grumpy Tissue

Dear Diary,
Today I was pulled out of my home to be spilt on by orange juice! But that wasn't the worst of it. After that I was put into the world's darkest place. But the good news was that I found some of my old pals, like Dr Pencil and Rude Rubber. However, I noticed that Rubber was a lot smaller than usual. One hour later, the dark place was tipped over and I was free for about 30 seconds, before a child picked me up. Of course, what's next is me being covered in snot. Well, you're right but who did it was a boy named Snotty Sam. Well if you really want to know what happens next my arm was pulled off. It wasn't just pulled off, it was eaten by a kid named Zoe, who put the rest of my body down the toilet. Well the next thing I knew I was shooting down a water slide and when I reached the bottom, I found a load of weird things down there so all I want to say is... help me!

Mia Franks (9)
St John The Baptist CE Primary School, Worthing

The Incredible Diary Of Juan The Lizard

Dear Diary,
What a day! This has been a crazy day. It all started when my owner took me to visit Barcelona. I was in a bag with a lot of stuff inside (and for some reason a needle and thread). After a little bit, I felt some cold air and I was wondering where it was coming from. That is when I saw there was a hole in the bottom corner. I knew I had to fix it so I got the needle and went to pack it up. But when I did my owner tripped and I fell out of the hole! When I got to my feet I could not see my owners. I knew if I told you how I was found this diary would be 91 pages long. So to make a long story short a man found me and somehow found my owners and if this experience has taught me anything... never try and fix a bag on a visit. Trust me, you will regret it.

Arthur Fitt (10)
St John The Baptist CE Primary School, Worthing

Ruby Enters A Fantasy World

Dear Diary,

My name is Ruby. Today at 10am I found this door hiding in my parents' room and I went through the door. It led me to this cool castle hallway. It looked so cool! It had cotton candy and lots of sweets.
"Welcome to our castle," said Rina the fairy and Princess Amelia.
I had so much fun. I went outside and I felt like it was a dream for a moment. "These are our unicorns," said the fairies.
I said, "I wish I could be one of you."
"Oh dear, it's very hard to be one of us," said the fairies and princesses.
I had a little party with the people in the town and then my time limit had finished so I looked for the door that led me here and went back home.
Finally, I went to bed.

Gaia Orecchia (7)
St John The Baptist CE Primary School, Worthing

The Girl's Adventure In Space

Dear Diary,
Back at school again! My teacher, Mrs Rose said our topic was space!
"No!"
"Yes!"
The other children didn't like space, just me. "What do you like space?" Rosie and Blue didn't like me but Henry the dog played with me.
I saw a rocket in the sky. The rocket picked me, Henry and Yuri. He took us to the moon. We were puzzled, curious and happy. I said, "When are we going home?"
We were on the moon. We put a flag on the moon. We were bouncing on the moon, it was fun. I enjoyed it with Henry and Yuri said, "One step for man, one leap for mankind!"
The adventure was over on the moon. When we got home we told our mum and dad about the adventure we had.

Nancy Hills (8)
St John The Baptist CE Primary School, Worthing

The Incredible Diary Of Me

Dear Diary,

Today I was thinking of when I moved house, from my old one to my new one. I was thinking of all my friends. I wondered if I would ever see them again and if I would ever talk to them. That made me feel very sad and unhappy. When we moved all our things were in a van. Mum tried to make me happy and excited but I was too scared. While we were there, Dad and me went to the café so my mum and sister could help with the moving men. I started to think if I would fit in or if I would make any friends. But now I know, I've made lots of friends and a best friend. Although I miss my old ones it is just how life goes, you can be best friends and then never see them again but I will always have them in my heart.

Emilie Greene (10)
St John The Baptist CE Primary School, Worthing

The Incredible Diary Of A Chair

Dear Diary,

Today I had the worst day of my life! First, it started off well, I was on top of the stack. Then it got so much worse. Some horrible child picked me up, held me in the air, swung me around and put me down as hard they could. It hurt my legs so, so badly. After that, the annoying boy reached into his pencil case, took out a Sharpie and started to scribble on me. He wouldn't stop. I tried to scream but nothing came out of my mouth. You wouldn't believe this but my day got even worse. The children were running, standing and jumping all over me then disaster struck. My legs collapsed underneath me. Realising I was no use to anyone I was picked and thrown in the corner of the classroom.

Flo Aguado (10)
St John The Baptist CE Primary School, Worthing

The Best Day Ever!

Dear Diary,
On Sunday I went to Brighton's stadium called the Amex. I was really excited. I got into the car and we drove. I was at the Amex! I got into my seat and I saw the players train and then the players went in to get ready for the match. I was really nervous but excited and the players walked on and I saw Mac Allister and March! It was Brighton vs Liverpool. The match started. Brighton almost scored a goal and the crowd said, "Oh!" But Liverpool scored a goal but Brighton scored an equaliser and the crowd said, "Yeahhhh!"
In the end, Mitoma scored a goal. At the end of the match I saw Mac Allister because Daddy arranged it for my birthday. It was the best day ever!

Harry Dicker (8)
St John The Baptist CE Primary School, Worthing

Freddie's Birthday Party

Dear Diary,
Yesterday, it was my friend's birthday party. He turned five and there were two bouncy castles, a cake and lots of party food. There was a tyre swing and this man pushed me on the swing. There was another swing but my legs were too long. I got a gift bag and it had bubbles, cake, a dinosaur mask and sweets like Haribos. One of the bouncy castles was a slide and the other one was a dinosaur one with two big dinosaur eggs in it and William (my brother) kept on jumping on it and kept on saying, "This is my baby!"

The cake was about one foot tall and there was a big number 5 candle and two dinosaurs and we all sang 'happy birthday' before he blew the candle out.

Isobel Harrex-Perks (8)
St John The Baptist CE Primary School, Worthing

The Incredible Diary Of Mr Sharp (A Grumpy Pencil)

Dear Diary,
What a day! To start off I got chewed by a child (he did not brush his teeth), I nearly passed out from the awful smell. When I was done being chewed, I was then finally sharpened but apparently, I was showing off about how sharp I was. That's why I have no friends but today a new pencil came out of the cupboard. That meant someone had to go into the big dark hole! It was dark, at first I could not see at all but I got used to it. I could not believe how much stationery was down there. Rubbers, pens, paper, rulers, whiteboard pens, Post-It notes and pencils.
Diary, please help me... Mr Sharp.

Harriet Brunton (10)
St John The Baptist CE Primary School, Worthing

The Incredible Diary Of Happy Disabled Hero

Dear Diary,

My day was exhausting. It all started when my mum was very ill. I thought she was dying. I am disabled and I can't even drive as I am too young. It looked like my mum was about to die so I dialled 999 using my mum's phone and she was healed. The people called me a hero and yesterday I saved an old lady from a high building. I kept on doing loads of hero stuff like saving a kitten from a fire (and people as well). I even met the mayor last week and was awarded a medal! As I was being presented with my award a fire broke out. I called the fire service so now everyone calls me The Disabled Hero.

Lillie Packham (10)
St John The Baptist CE Primary School, Worthing

Jack Grealish

Dear Diary,

Oh my goodness, I can't believe I won the Treble. The year is 2023. We won three types of cups which were the Premier League, FA Cup and the Champions League. My name is Jack Grealish. I play for England and Man City. I am 27 years old. I support Villa and then City. First we won the FA Cup then it was the Premier League, the last was the Champions League. That was when Man City won their first Champions League. In the FA Cup we beat Man United so we could win. It was 2-1 to us. It was 1-0 to us when we were playing the final for the Premier League. It was against Chelsea. It was 1-0 to us in the Champions League final. We were against Inter. This made us win the treble. We were so happy. Man United won the treble in 1998 so now we've both won it, the Treble. This has made history for Man City.

Frankie Brookes (10)
St Peter's Catholic Primary School, Bartley Green

Never Be Seen Again

Dear Diary,
Wow! What an amazing view. The sky was covered in a thick blue blanket as I started to invade, taking over like a river's banks, beautiful. The humongous, beautiful sky changed instantly into a gloomy ark sending terror into the sky. Would you be scared? I rapidly sent blinding bright beams down onto the people of Japan, ready to pick my next victims. *Which ones?* I think to myself as I searched high and low. The excitement ran through my body as the sun started to set on the horizon. In the far but near distance, there was a small creature I believed was called a human. They had an odd appearance and I was freaked out. I watched the terror fill their faces as I slowly picked who would be my friend. It was day 103459 of my own and days were getting longer and thoughts started to rush into my head like a race car rushing around a track. The smooth iron walls bored me. I just wanted a friend. Why were they scared? Was it my neon green, slimy body that scared them or was it my massive, monster spaceship that scared them? The disappointment started to take over me

and I lost hope, thinking I would be alone forever. I zoomed off into the distance and would never be seen by humans again.

Connie Mcintosh (8)
St Peter's Catholic Primary School, Bartley Green

The Diary Of A Happy Girl

Dear Diary,

Today I was finally made one of the Caritas Ambassadors of my school. This has been my dream since it came into existence in my school. I was afraid to apply because I hate to be rejected but my mum encouraged me to go after my heart and forget about failure and that there's no harm in trying. I am a Caritas Ambassador today and this is a dream come true.

Although I am on a trial period with some of my friends who applied. But I hope I meet the requirements at the end of the trial period. I would be so proud of myself if this came to pass as I love to support my school and the community physically or in another way I can. I will pray and work hard towards this dream and I am definitely going to come back to tell you how it went. Today is my best day!

Mitchell Nwokolo (9)
St Peter's Catholic Primary School, Bartley Green

Diary Of Spider-Man

Dear Diary,
It's Peter Parker, aka Spider-Man, and I'm sitting down to write in you after an eventful day. Life as a superhero is never dull and today was no exception. There are so many thoughts running through my mind and I feel like I have the guts to tell you about my life as a superhero. Being Spider-Man is like a curse and blessing, like one time I had to save a train with my web power and it ripped my suit. It was so painful. There's too much pressure being a hero but with great power comes great responsibility, as Uncle Ben used to say.
As the day progressed, I found myself tackling various crimes throughout the city, stopping crimes, it's like a little kindness.
It is time to finish the diary now, bye.

Aldrin Diljo (9)
St Peter's Catholic Primary School, Bartley Green

The Day My Friend Didn't Want To Do PE

Dear Diary,

Yesterday was the most crazy day of my life. Let me explain... So we went on this trip to the training athletic stadium and Miss Tucksnik told us to get in pairs. Me and my best friend looked straight into each other's eyes, darted towards each other and became partners. After five minutes we got on a bus. Get this, everyone but my friend, who I was sitting with, had their PE kits in their bags. My friend Meika had a cushion. Nobody knows why but she did. I asked why and she replied, "I don't want to do PE!" I was shocked. But that was it and I will let you know if anything else happens.

Jorgie Bullock (9)
St Peter's Catholic Primary School, Bartley Green

How Jade Got Her Heavenly Voice

Dear Diary,
It is 2022 and two years ago my voice was hoarse and terrible. In 2020 my voice was very rough and hideous. It took me two years to get a good voice. I practised every day non-stop. I got bullied when I went out because I sang to the songs being played. I couldn't take it so I practised every single day. Come 2021 my voice was better, much better. I still practised but didn't get bullied so much. I got better and better. Then, when I tried a new note, I... did... it! I was really proud.
Moral of my story: Never give up because I didn't and look where I am now... Famous and happy!

Meika Ivy-Georgia Foote (9)
St Peter's Catholic Primary School, Bartley Green

Cup Winners!

Dear Diary,

Yesterday was the best day of my life! I woke up feeling nervous but excited at the same time. We were in the final of the French football tournament.

My team and I sang songs all the way there on the coach, trying to distract ourselves from thinking of the match. On our arrival at the football stadium, we changed into our football kits and warmed up. The game went so fast the score was 7-6 to us. It was so tense but I scored the winning goal. I was so proud of myself and my teammates. We sang louder on the way back then we did on the way there. I was very tired and I finally fell asleep.

Maisie Bullock (9)
St Peter's Catholic Primary School, Bartley Green

My Holiday

Dear Diary,

Last weekend I went to Cornwall. I did a lot. It started with my mother who had to get a hire car. Then it was a five-hour drive! We got there late. I had dinner and went to the beach which was really close to us. We only had to walk there. After, we went to bed. After the Golden Sunrise we went to the beach for the day. We played cricket. Then we went to the Bluff Inn for lunch. We spent the night at a carnival and after that we went to bed. The next morning we drove back home. It was Father's Day when we got back.

That's all for today, Archie.

Archie Strange (9)
St Peter's Catholic Primary School, Bartley Green

A Day In A Life Of A Pet Dog

Dear Diary,
It was a nice sunny day and my pack family were bustling about. They were taking drinks and food. *Where are they going?* My pack left me thinking I would stay in my bed all day but really I sneaked out by the flap in the door and I played with my friends. But I had to be back before my pack came back. I was excited to see my friends and play with them. Then sadly I had to stop playing and go back home before my pack got home.
Talk to you soon, Kitty the dog.

Eva Beale (9)
St Peter's Catholic Primary School, Bartley Green

The Mascot Exprience

Dear Diary,

I started the day off by eating my breakfast, brushing my teeth and putting my kit on. I drove to Villa Park and walked through the crowded stadium with the other mascots. I was so excited and then there I was face-to-face with the Aston Villa players. Then we walked onto the pitch. The game was fantastic... Aston Villa won 4-0. I was so happy. I've got to end there... I'll catch up with you later, Diary.

Alfie Boffey (9)

St Peter's Catholic Primary School, Bartley Green

Riley Oddberry's Day Out
An extract

Dear Diary,
Today was the freakiest day ever. I went on a school trip with my class (and my buddy, Jacob). Now every school trip goes wrong for me. I always get expelled. My name is Riley Oddberry, I'm in Year 6. I've been expelled from five schools! So, we went to the art gallery, it was bla bla bla but I was on my best behaviour so I didn't have to go to a different school. My classmate, Jo Cole hates me so much but my big problem is that Jo is my headteacher's favourite student.
Jo came up to me and started putting nuts in Jacob's hair. I stood up to protect him but he told me to sit back down and stop worrying. "I like nuts!" he said.
I don't remember touching Jo but when I opened my eyes he was sitting in the fountain shouting, "Riley pushed me!"
Miss David came over and said, "That's it, Mr Oddberry!"
Jacob stood up and said, "I pushed him, Miss!"
"I am sorry Mr Lee but I think Oddberry pushed Jo."

When Miss turned around Jacob gave me a tired look. "Follow me, now!"
I went with her further into the art gallery. When we got to the back she said to me that I'd been very bad and causing problems. "Mr Oddberry, you've been expelled from five schools so you have to be careful what you do."
Her black jacket melted into black feathery wings, her legs turned blue and she grew a long, spiky tail. She or 'it' got ready to attack but my Latin teacher, Mr Hambleton threw me a ruler (how would that help?!). I turned it over, tapped it three times and it turned into a sword!...

Anna Rocher (10)
The Herne Junior School, Petersfield

The Diary Of Pote

Dear Diary,

Today was interesting. To my surprise a large crimson-red portal appeared in the sky. Green humans fell, landing on the hard grey concrete. Everyone began to scream and run.

Me and my friends watched in horror as the disease spread like a wave, washing over the world. The apocalypse had begun. I didn't know what to do.

Me and my friends wandered around trying to avoid as many zombies as possible. It was so difficult because every human on Earth is now a zombie. We don't know how it had spread like wildfire. We had to build a base to stay in so we gathered wood and found a huge oak tree in a park. We assembled a treehouse. We grabbed our belongings and moved in. It was hard. Very hard. We were only children and boom, the world was filled with zombies. We had to look after ourselves now with no adults.

Later that day we went out to see what had happened. There was still the red portal in the sky, but it was blue now. If we could find a way up there we could find what caused it and reverse it back but it was probably 150 metres in the air.

All the zombies gathered in one place. A tree. Our tree. We ran away as we dried our salty tears. That tree house had our last memories of our beloved parents. Pictures, notebooks and flowers, all gone because of those destructive zombies.

We'll get them back someday because of the incident. We'll build a base in a house, nice and protected. We all felt so tired. With every blink of an eye, our eyelids felt heavier. We got into our comfortable beds not knowing what was to come...

Milo De Giovanni (10)
The Herne Junior School, Petersfield

The Death Of A Hero
An extract

Dear Diary,
Hello fellow Athenians, it is I, Aegeus, Theseus' dad. Now, I know you're thinking that I'm dead, well I am dead, but up in Heaven you can do everything that you can do down there, in the underworld as we people up here call it. Well, a couple of days ago, I travelled back in time (yes, we can travel back in time, no big deal) to see what really happened to my mighty son. I will tell you what happened but if there's any cruel Cretian people reading this diary, please slap this diary out of their hands because they're smelly and unkind! Here we go... A long time ago, in a period long before Jesus was born lived two rival cities, Crete and Athens. They were such rivals that Crete declared war on Athens many times. Yet when Athens fought back, they called it a draw many times. But Pasiphae (Minos' wife) gave birth to a foul-smelling, ugly beast. And they named it... The Minotaur. As this half-man, half-bull grew up, it grew to be a really strong individual. So Minos had to hire Aaedalus (an engineer) to build a maze for this beast to live in and he called it 'The Labyrinth'.

When they released the beast into the Labyrinth it sat at the doorway for days, charging at the huge metal door that stood at the start, with breathtaking architecture.
It took a couple of days before the Minotaur ventured off into the maze. He then found his way into the centre of the Labyrinth. He lay there for hours on end but the evil King Minos came up with a plan to put his beast of a son to use...

Barney Bryant (10)
The Herne Junior School, Petersfield

The School Of Weirdness

An extract

Dear Diary,

Today was the weirdest day ever. It all started when... Actually I should probably tell you my name first, so my name is Evie Williams and I go to St Junior School. My school is weirder than weird. I'm new, I've only been here for about three weeks. I've made a lot of friends since I moved here, my house is the only place I can relax, have a break and do what I want, it's like my happy place. So let's start... As I said I'm new. My teacher, Mrs Barnaby, showed me around. And I even have my own locker. Guess what my number is? You can't, I'll tell you, it's 826. My classroom is called 'The Alien Apocalypse'! I put a lot of stuff in my locker, like my bag and a bunch of pictures from home. The classroom is okay. Our first task was to find the red ruby. I thought this was odd for my first task, but little did I know what our second task was. I had to get through the first one first! I looked everywhere or at least I thought I did. I thought someone had already found it since they'd been here longer. As I said, our first mission is to find the red ruby. I already told you I felt I'd looked everywhere and someone else found it. I looked,

looked and looked. I pushed a door open, it slammed open, surprisingly there was a secret library. I looked for a book on the ruby. I found books about emeralds, crystals, gold, but no ruby. About two hours later I found it!

Chloe Williams (10)
The Herne Junior School, Petersfield

Me, A Politician?

Dear Diary,

Today was one of the days where I made an amazing achievement. You see, it all started a few days ago in our little flat in London. My mum said that instead of our normal extra-large Hawaiian pizza that was divided between me, my sister, my brother and my parents, we would be getting a tiny own-brand cheese pizza! I realised this was because money was tight. I had heard my parents saying stuff like 'inflation', 'Ukraine', 'government', 'annoying' and 'tax'. After eating the pizza (it was disgusting), I decided to write a letter to my local MP and ask what he thought. I got a reply soon after saying I could try helping out at a food bank. He also claimed I had a brilliant political mind and should consider joining the Children's Parliament. I asked and they said yes! I decided to try and help stop the cost of living crisis. So I set up a charity with the help of the Children's Parliament. They decided to name it Amelie's Foodbank, after me! And today was the day when we finally finished setting up a food bank in almost every English school! I truly believe one day, inflation will be halted.

Leela Sheridan-Maan (10)
The Herne Junior School, Petersfield

Spooky Cottage

Dear Diary,

I am writing to you as I am nearly at Spooky Cottage. It is beginning to grow darker and my bones ache, but I'm not turning back now. After a few more minutes, I stood staring at the ancient moss-covered building, mouth open in shock. The ripped curtains, the musty red door hinged open and the whisper of the darkness. Was I really doing this? I opened the door and ventured inside. As darkness swallowed around me, I lit a flame. To my horror, blood spilt across the floor, glass shattered everywhere. Now this wasn't just a haunted house, this was a crime scene. I turned around and ran...

Megan Llewelyn-Williams (10)
The Herne Junior School, Petersfield

Dreamland Adventure

Dear Diary,
What a day I've had! It all began whilst going to school with my BFFs, Maisy and William. Suddenly, as we turned into Verity Lane, there was silence instead of the usual birds tweeting. I thought that I was imagining things, but I saw Maisy sprinting around the neighbourhood and decided I would rather get detention and figure out what was going on than get to school without figuring out about it. I hesitated for just a few seconds and heard a voice. I was convinced that it was Maisy's and sprinted after William. When I caught up with him, I spotted that Maisy wasn't there! "William! Where's Maisy?" I yelled.
William shrugged. I scanned the surrounding area and spotted an unusual sight. A building that had caved in. *Wait! Caved in! Oh no! Maisy could be inside it! We better help her! And quick!* I thought. Later!

Aiko Wilkoszewska (9)
Wyborne Primary School, New Eltham

A Bug's Horrific Day In The Museum

Dear Diary,
What a day... I'm still shaking like jelly! Let me tell you why. I was in my block minding my own business when four beastly small humans approached me. Their fingernails were as sharp as four knives stabbing my block. Their smiles gave me nightmares. Although the worst thing was they started stacking me and my friends like the Leaning Tower of Pisa. Our faces were banged several times on the table. We have concussion, all eighteen of us! We were thrown against the walls so many times it is impossible to count every time! Tell us good luck tomorrow, we are going to 100% need it, no doubt. Humans! We were here first. Outrageous, absolutely outrageous! I'm totally speechless and I don't have any other words other than for this diary!

Lottie Franklin (10)
Wyborne Primary School, New Eltham

The Diary Of An Evil Queen

Dear Diary,

Infuriating! I hate that stupid girl! She is the reason I am in this place... Snow White. The worst person in the world. If you can even call her that! She is barely even human.

It all started when I tried to murder her (for the second time). I got caught and sent to jail. Now all I have is a toothbrush, a diary and a stupid newspaper to see what all the royals have been up to whilst I'm stuck and stranded, left staring out of the barred windows, waiting to be set free.

Everyone calls me 'The Evil Queen'. I'm just misunderstood. If they want an evil queen they will get one. I'll show them, I'll show them all! They'll see the true evil queen shine!

Reina, the 'evil' former queen.

Danielle Tinnion (10)
Wyborne Primary School, New Eltham

The Bomb Dropped

Dear Diary,
I didn't have much time. My train was coming, it was time to say goodbye as my mum and dad disappeared from the platform. *What number are you?* I thought when looking at the boy next to me. *Wait, stop, I may never see my parents again.* I thought I was going to Canada so I would at least go to the beach every day I'm there.
When I opened the door there stood an old grumpy man in the dark with a deep voice. "Are you going to come in? Hang up your coat!"
From that moment, I knew that today would be an interesting day. "Where should I put my bag?" "Over there."
When I walked into the room I couldn't believe what I saw...

Taysia Weston-Lawson (9)
Wyborne Primary School, New Eltham

My Amazing Diary, Thursday 13th 2078

An extract

Dear Diary,
I woke up this morning to see rain. Holographic rain. I got dressed and grabbed my cyber glasses. I ran downstairs and grabbed my breakfast. I thanked my robot butler and ran down to my garage. I had a debate about if I should go in my hover car or use my hoverboard. It ended up being my hover car and I turned on self-drive to get me to school. My school is a massive building, bigger than a skyscraper. It makes up for all the robots learning here. The bottom floors are for humans, floors 1-20. Then floors 20-40 are for the robots learning how to take over our jobs. I find AI weird... I walked in and used my hover boots to get up the long stairs up to floor 15. I finally got up but the corridor was long like usual. I again used my hover boots to zoom through the corridor like Flash. I finally got to my class. Class 309. I walked in to see everyone waiting for me. They looked off today... I sat down next to my BFF, Koli. She also seemed off. We learned nothing because our teacher's an AI bot... She just stood there out of battery. I used my

cyber glasses to look at her stats and it said she was fully charged. It felt like the day should be over but it's only 12...
After lunch I had to walk to class since my hover boots were out of charge... but I charged them through the night... After walking for ages we learned nothing again. I walked home and my robot butler was just standing there, like every AI today...

Jessica Clements
Ysgol Gynradd Gymraeg Caerffili, Caerphilly

Diary Of A Fairy Kid

Dear Diary,
This is my first entry and today was my birthday. I am 11 now which means I got my first wand! I woke up really early because my pet unicorn, Candy, was hungry so I had to go out and feed her some sugar cubes. My name is Forest by the way. I live at 33 Mushroom Way. I have a younger brother called Leaf. After I fed Candy I did my makeup and went downstairs to wait for my parents and Leaf to come down so I put the TV on. After an hour or two Mum, Dad and Leaf came down for breakfast which was French toast with chocolate then I got to open my presents. As well as my first wand I got a new saddle bag for candy and a new phone. Then I flew over to the park where I met my best friend, Lilac. We joked around for a while but then she had to go home so I walked home with her because we both live on the same street. It was already lunch by the time I arrived back and in our house if it is your birthday you can choose what is for lunch. I picked pixie pears and milk with honey because it's my favourite food and for dessert we had banana sorbet which was delicious. Later we all went out to the crystal mines. I found five made, ten amethyst and fifteen opals. I love crystals. Most

people think it's weird I prefer gemstones to buttons but I don't care really. After that, we just chilled out for the rest of the day.
Goodnight, Forrest.

Molly Jones (9)
Ysgol Gynradd Gymraeg Caerffili, Caerphilly

My Amazing Diary
An extract

Dear Diary,

It's two days before prom. I have my shoes and dress ready and am extremely excited. In just a couple of days I'm going to see Harry Styles perform live in Cardiff and then I'm going on holiday. I can't wait to go to Croatia... lying in the sun, in and out of the pools. Ahh, I just can't wait for that summer breeze. Normally I would start to pack by now but as I get older I realise there is no need to start packing 12 days before. I am only allowed to take a certain amount of clothes because we are flying. I did consider wearing three layers so I could bring more in my suitcase but then realised I would be boiling hot. The only problem is, one of my cats named Wilbur isn't coming back home. As I go to bed tonight this could be the sixth night he hasn't come back. And before we leave we must take our two French bulldogs to the kennels so that they are safe. When we get there we aren't able to go straight to our caravan because the people still there will be packing and leaving. And in order to get to the airport we will have to drive up to Birmingham and then to Liverpool, then we will stay the night in a Premier Inn and then wake up at 4am to be at the airport by 5 and fly at 7.

When we arrive we cannot go straight to the caravan so we will hire a car and then just chill on the beach...

Alessandra Winter
Ysgol Gynradd Gymraeg Caerffili, Caerphilly

8/5/2018

Dear Diary,
OMG! Today was so exhilarating. I went shark caging. This is the best vacation ever! I thought taking a trip to Hawaii would be idiotic considering the temperature but this has been the best week of my life! First, we went on a giant speed boat and drove into the middle of the sea. Secondly, they gave us some rules. No diving without an oxygen tank, no putting your fingers out of the cage, and no jumping in without being told to. Third, they gave us our suits, they were a bit tight but it was okay. Then they lowered the cage, the bars looked skeletal! That's when I went in. I waved goodbye like it was time for me to die. Finally, they lowered me and my mum in. Seeing all those sharks was so cool! I hope we go again!
See you tomorrow!

Tyra-Jae Taylor
Ysgol Gynradd Gymraeg Caerffili, Caerphilly

Young Writers Information

We hope you have enjoyed reading this book – and that you will continue to in the coming years.

If you're the parent or family member of an enthusiastic poet or story writer, do visit our website **www.youngwriters.co.uk/subscribe** and sign up to receive news, competitions, writing challenges and tips, activities and much, much more! There's lots to keep budding writers motivated!

If you would like to order further copies of this book, or any of our other titles, then please give us a call or order via your online account.

Young Writers
Remus House
Coltsfoot Drive
Peterborough
PE2 9BF
(01733) 890066
info@youngwriters.co.uk

Join in the conversation!
Tips, news, giveaways and much more!

YoungWritersUK YoungWritersCW youngwriterscw

Scan me to watch The Incredible Diary Of video!